HIDE

LINDA ARENA

Author's Tranquility Press
ATLANTA, GEORGIA

Copyright © 2024 by Linda Arena

All rights reserved. No part of this publication may be reproduced, distributed or transmitted in any form or by any means, including photocopying, recording, or other electronic or mechanical methods, without the prior written permission of the publisher, except in the case of brief quotations embodied in critical reviews and certain other noncommercial uses permitted by copyright law. For permission requests, write to the publisher, addressed "Attention: Permissions Coordinator," at the address below.

Linda Arena/Author's Tranquility Press
3900 N Commerce Dr. Suite 300 #1255
Atlanta, GA 30331, USA
www.authorstranquilitypress.com

Ordering Information:
Quantity sales. Special discounts are available on quantity purchases by corporations, associations, and others. For details, contact the "Special Sales Department" at the address above.

Hide/Linda Arena
Hardback: 978-1-964362-71-7
Paperback: 978-1-964362-03-8
eBook: 978-1-964362-04-5

Dedication

"I dedicate this book to:
Rachael Cantu
And
Kathie Bludworth
who are the two best cheerleaders
I've ever, ever had."

Contents

Chapter One The Escape 1

Chapter Two Haunted 12

Chapter Three Hope 17

Chapter Four The Search 37

Chapter Five Horace Hamilton 43

Chapter Six Captured 62

Chapter Seven The Offer 69

Chapter Eight Hopkins 81

Chapter Nine Clive's Revenge 88

Chapter Ten Discovery 93

Chapter Eleven Wolf Hunt 99

Chapter Twelve The Wedding 113

Chapter Thirteen The Judge 136

Chapter Fourteen The Hunt for Megan 150

Chapter Fifteen The Marketplace 161

Chapter Sixteen Leaving for Florida 171

Chapter Seventeen Florida 178

Chapter Eighteen The Takedown 194

Chapter Nineteen Recovery 198

Chapter Twenty Ten Years Later 205

Chapter Twenty-One The Abduction 214
Chapter Twenty-Two Buried 221
Chapter Twenty-Three El Guardo's 225

Chapter One
The Escape

Pouring coffee from a lunch box thermos, nine-year-old Megan Hollis, a precocious little girl whose violet eyes carried the weight of the world, filled her dad's favorite mug. Carefully, she set it down on the handmade table trying desperately not to spill a single drop.

Today, she thought. He will come today. She set the thermos back on the shelf and returned to her seat. The coffee cup was jiggling.

"Daddy, are you here?" Her eyes frantically searched the small playroom, looking for any sign that he indeed was here. At that moment, she felt a slight tug on her skirt. "It is you!" tug…

"I've been waiting a whole year for you to come. Did you have to go away for work?" tug…tug … Her eyes widened for a split second, but she continued, "Did you have to go to school?" *tug*… "What did you study in school daddy?" Silence…. "Must be a big secret if you can't tell me." *tug…tug…* "Did you like your teacher? *tug*…. "Did you have recess.?" *tug*…

The intercom buzzed, Natalie's voice called out, "Megan…" Hearing the sound of his wife's voice took him by surprise and he gasped.

"Yes Mommy, guess what? Daddy's here! He came to see us and I'm so happy! Remember how you said you talked to him?"

"Yes baby, I do…"

"I think that's what he's doing now, only with tugs on my skirt, one tug for yes, two tugs for no!"

Natalie slumped against the wall. Her beautiful baby, so imaginative and determined to believe that someone could return from the dead. I wish I had never told her that he could and would come back. "That's wonderful baby…um, I must go to the grocery. I'll be right back, ten minutes tops, ok? Will you be alright while I'm gone?"

"Yes Mommy…Daddy's here, I'll be fine."

"Remember…"

Megan interrupted her, "Yes Mommy…I know hide, if someone comes…"

"Okay…" She got into her car and drove toward town.

Within seconds, gunfire erupted and there was an explosion. Megan felt a pull on her shirt. "Do I hide, daddy?" **tug…** "Okay! I'm afraid, daddy!"

Megan ran to the corner that butted against the house and pushed the panel open. Quickly, she crawled inside and slammed the panel closed. And just like she'd been taught, she crawled over to the mattress, covered herself with the handmade quilt.

Garrett left and went toward the sound of the explosion. Sure enough, it was Natalie's car. Those bastards! He went back to Megan as fast as he could. He tried to sit down but he wasn't heavy enough.

Within minutes, the sound of heavy footfalls could be heard on the stairs outside. Doors slammed open, furniture thrown against the walls, and windows breaking.

Megan began crying softly. **tug…tug…** She instantly quieted.

A harsh voice said right outside her door! "Where is that little brat? The mother said she was down here."

Another voice said, "How should I know? She isn't here, now."

"Okay, we'll catch her when she's brought back. Let's go."

The heavy boots disappeared, and she was left in silence. She whispered, "Mommy where are you?" **tug…tug…** "Did those bad men hurt her? Daddy! Did they?" **tug…** Megan cried into the quilt to muffle her sobs. "Is she dead?" **tug…** Megan collapsed, and her dad covered her up.

Sleep my sweet baby while you can, thought Garret Hollis, because I'm sure they have us surrounded.

Doctor Clive Jenkins sat across the street staring at the Hollis house. He was well hidden in a small stand of trees. He thought, *how can one small girl get away from us? And who is helping her? Her mother and father are dead. So, who's left? Her file states that the Hollis's adopted her when she was only days old. Garret and Natalie lived a solitary life, with no relatives. So, who?*

Dialing his phone, he waited impatiently for Jerry to answer, finally he answered "Hey Jerry, dig deeper into the Hollis family and find out if they have a cousin, or neighbors that could be considered close friends. Anyone that would risk their life to hide her."

"Sure boss."

After several hours of waiting without so much as a leaf rustling. He thought *she wasn't coming back. Hell, she's probably long gone. So now what?* Looking at his watch, it was well after midnight. *I'm done, I'll start over tomorrow.*

***

Megan began to stir. Instantly, Garret tugged on her shirt for reassurance. He did not want her to wake up and have her think she was alone. *Footsteps!* Several people were walking beside the house in the direction of the road! *They're leaving!*

"Wake up Megan, *come* on baby, wake up!" He tried to shake her, but of course, to no avail. "Megan, we need to get away from here now!"

"Daddy, you're too cold!" **tug…tug…** "Move away. I'm freezing." **tug…tug…** "Why not?" She sat up.

He moved away from her. *Great*! Pulling on her shirt, he attempted to drag her out of the safe room; she didn't understand. Grabbing hold of the shirt as hard as he could, he yanked. The shirt moved!

"Daddy, do you want me to leave here?" **tug…** "Are the bad men gone?" **tug…** "Ok, I need the bathroom first." **tug…** "Daddy, do I need my go bag?" **tug…**

The go bag! How could I have forgotten? We put an emergency backpack together that contained everything she would need for several days.

Megan came back from the bathroom and grabbed her go bag. "OK, Daddy, I'm ready." They snuck out the side door and ran for the woods. Garrett kept ahold of her shirt so he could direct her down the path.

We chose Broken Arrow because it was a small village. Everybody knows each other and if a stranger enters town, in five minutes, they all know it. This time, Natalie must not have had any warning. Although we were fortunate enough to be able to stay here for four years, now we have to go.

My beautiful, beautiful Natalie gone; blown up by those bastards! Garrett stopped as the mere thought of her dying struck him, and he was paralyzed in grief.

"Daddy, what's wrong?" **no tug…** "Are you still here?" **tug…** "Are we lost?" **tug…tug…** "Are you sad?" **tug…** "Me too, daddy, me too. Can we sit down for just a minute?" **tug…** Megan sat down on the ground and began to cry; Garrett let her have her moment.

When she had no more tears, she stood up. "Okay, daddy I'm ready." **tug…**

After they walked for a several miles, he felt safe enough to stop for a while, suddenly they heard, a low growl not fifty yards away…wolf!

Garrett, frantically, looked in all directions. Megan, on the other hand, was perfectly calm. "He won't hurt us daddy, so don't be afraid."

"How do you know that?" Garrett yelled, knowing full well she couldn't hear him.

"Because I can feel his heart. His heart says friend not foe."

Interesting, he thought, how does someone hear a heart?

"I know you don't understand, but that's okay." She paused, "You know dad, I can hear you when you speak."

The stunned Garrett asked, "Wait, you can hear me?"

Megan smiled, "When you talk, yes, but you don't have a shirt for me to tug on."

"Cute, Megan. How long have you been able to do this?"

"Always…"

Garrett thought, was this gift of hers something I knew about in life? Maybe, if so, do you forget some things after you die? I don't know.

Grrrr… closer this time.

"Daddy, I'm sleepy."

"I can't leave you with that wolf prowling around."

"Yes, you can! I told you. He won't hurt me. I promise he won't."

The one thing he did remember was that if Megan said something was true: it was. "Okay then, I'm going to look for shelter. See that fallen tree?" Megan nodded. "Go over there and rest while I'm gone. If anyone comes fall behind it. They won't be able to see you behind there. I won't be long."

"Okay…" Megan walked over to the smaller end of the tree and sat down. Within two minutes, she lay atop the tree trunk and fell fast asleep.

Crunch, crunch, soft footsteps approached. Closer now, crunch.

"Grrrr!" Hazel sniffed. She looked at Mazey, a human!

Mazey sniffed and agreed, female. Sniffing the air there wasn't another human scent nearby. They approached cautiously and slowly so not to startle the child.

Hazel's eyes widened when the howling began. Mazey nuzzled Megan until she stirred.

Megan recognized the urgency in the wolves' eyes, and with a bit of muzzle prodding, she finally understood to get on Mazey's back. She wrapped her arms around Mazey's neck, as she slid off the tree trunk.

* * *

Garrett was so frustrated that he turned in rapid circles, kicking up small leaf whirlwinds. He failed miserably to find a safe place for Megan. There was not one cabin, or lean too, or a small cave in the whole area. So, without looking further, he headed back to where he left Megan; she could be awake by now. As he approached the fallen tree, it only took one glance to realize that she was not there. *No…no….!* Scouring every inch of where he left her, there wasn't a single clue as to where she'd gone or with who. What happened to make her leave? He swirled in circles, looking for a direction to go in. But found that he did not even know which way to go. *I've lost her. Now what?*

He didn't know how long he had sat there beating himself up for leaving her alone. As time went on, he convinced himself to give up the search. Suddenly, he heard a low whimper close by and looked up. Laying twenty feet away, on the path was the largest wolf he'd ever seen. *He seems to be looking directly at me!*

"Do you know where Megan is?"

The wolf stood up and headed down the path, he turned back and whimpered. Garrett ran to the wolf, "Show me where she is."

They ran only a half-a-mile before he heard the men's voices in front of them. The wolf darted into the brush and laid down. Garrett, on the other hand, ran right over to them and listened in.

"I'm tired," said the dark-haired man. "We've been out here for hours."

"Yes, four to be exact, and if we don't find the girl, we'll be more than tired."

"I know, the doctor was clear, find her or else."

Doctor! What doctor? **What doctor!** screamed Garrett.

"We better get moving. Suddenly, I'm freezing," said the big burly man and he began vigorously rubbing his arms to generate warmth.

As the two men walked away Garrett tried to stop them. But he had no idea how. He tried blocking their path, but they just walked right through him. Although, he was happy to see that they had a slight shiver as they did so. *There's nothing I can do here. I've gotta get to Megan.*

Once the two men disappeared into the woods, he went back to the wolf. *Okay, boy, take me to Megan.*

They wove through thick under growth until they came upon a ten-by-ten-foot clearing. The wolf laid down panting heavily. Poor guy, he's worn out.

I'll let him rest awhile while I scout the woods nearby. Maybe we're close, he thought. Soaring upwards to about thirty feet high, he looked between the trees for a well-traveled footpath or trampled brush. He found nothing, so he went back to where the wolf lay. He was barely breathing! This guy is dying!

Garrett soared upward and screamed, "Megan if you can hear me, this wolf is dying. I'm sure you're with the wolves because this one came to get me. But now he is in real trouble and needs your help. Repeating this mantra several times, he went back to sit with the wolf.

Sitting down as best he could, he ran his hands over the wolf. The wolf moaned, so he continued. As he petted the wolf, he began to understand that his hands were cold and felt good. He must be feverish, probably so.

After a few minutes, he heard howling. Garrett leapt up and began to yell, "Over here! We're over here!"

First to break through the brush were a pair of extremely large wolves and then Megan. "Daddy, are you here?" **Tug.**

Her eyes immediately shifted to the wolf and ran to his side. "Oh no, Loki!" She buried her face deep into his furry chest. Her words were low and garbled.

Garrett wanted to hear what she was saying but he couldn't. It almost sounded like a foreign language. I'll ask her later, right now her whole focus was on the wolf.

Five minutes later, she sat up and rocked back on her knees. It was obvious that she'd been crying. She wiped her face with her dress and leaned over the wolf again. This time she doubled up her fist and smacked the wolf on the top of his head. His eyes opened and he appeared startled as he rolled up on his sternum.

"He'll be fine now, daddy. I fixed him."

Yes, you did, Megan. Yes… **you** did.

Howling could be heard to the right while others sounded farther away coming from several different directions.

"We have to leave here," whispered Megan. "Follow us, daddy."

They disappeared into the brush, and Garrett was about to follow them, when he noticed that the wolf called Loki didn't move.

"Megan, Loki is not moving! Megan, can you hear me?"

"Yes, I can." Megan burst through the brush and laid her hand on Loki's head. "Loki, you must go home now. Find Mazey, she wants to see you."

The wolf stood up and headed toward the den; Megan and I followed.

Once Garrett knew Megan was safely hidden. He decided to explore the surrounding area. There must be a reason why these wolves are so upset.

He headed toward the closest wolf sound and ran right through a man crouching by a fallen tree. Garrett and the man were both startled for different reasons. The man jumped up and began brushing himself off as if trying to dislodge spider webs. Garrett was just startled but took his time in checking the guy over. *I must find out who this guy is and why he's looking for Megan.*

The guy was tall and slender. And didn't look like a foot soldier at all. So, who are they?

Garrett yelled at the guy. "What do you want?"

"I don't want nothing, dude."

"You can hear me?"

"Yeah, I can hear you. You're yelling loud enough."

"Interesting. Why are you looking for my daughter?"

"I doubt that you're her father because he is dead."

"True, I still want to know what you want with her."

"I don't know. The doctor just said. Get her. In fact, she would be better off with the doctor, her mother is a real piece of work. Drunk all the time and whoring with every guy she that would give her money. Hey, where are you? I can't see you. Come out of the bushes."

"I'm not in the bushes, I'm standing right beside you."

"No, you're not. I could see you if you were."

"Well, you can't, because I'm Megan's father! And, the whore's husband, jackass."

"Yeah, right, dude. And I'm the Queen of England."

Garrett reached out and grabbed his arm. The coldness of his touch made the guy shiver from head to toe.

"Can you feel that?" he screamed. "That's me touching you!"

The expression on the guy's face was priceless. Shock and horror all rolled into one! And he turned around and ran shrieking into the woods.

Garrett wanted desperately to punch him in the face, but he couldn't. Something went horribly wrong after I died. I need to find out what it was. Hopefully, Megan can shed some light on what happened to her mother after I died.

He was surprised he found his way back to the den so easily and called for Megan to come out.

A disheveled, filthy little girl appeared before him. His heart broke. "Hey baby girl, how are you doing?"

"Are we leaving? I brought my 'go' bag!"

"Not yet, sorry honey. But I do need to talk to you for a few minutes. Okay?"

"Sure daddy…"

"Tell me how your mom was, after I died."

"She cried a lot mostly. Is that what you mean?"

"Yes, did she go into town?"

"Not at first, after a while she did. It seemed like she got really mad at me."

"Why would you think that?"

"I tried to be so good, really I did, but she made me sleep in my playroom every night."

Garrett was horrified. "You didn't sleep in your bed in the house?"

"No, just in the playroom. But now I know it wasn't me that made her mad, cause I heard her going down the stairs and leaving every night."

Desperate to hide his disgust, "Did she bring friends home?"

"Oh yes! She had lots of friends over. Lots of dancing and laughing. Mostly, they must have had really good food cause she moaned a lot."

"Moaned?"

"Yeah, happy moans like when your hamburger tastes extra good."

"Thanks, baby. Now we need to clean you up. Let's find a river."

Garrett was upset, his beautiful wife must have had to resort to prostitution to feed them. That's the only logical explanation that makes sense. He shook his head; their meager savings would have run out rather quickly.

Chapter Two
Haunted

Dr. Jenkins' cellphone rang. The caller's ID read Hopkins! *Finally, some news about the girl,* he thought, *at least it better be.*

"Hopkins, tell me some good news."

"I don't know how good it is, but I did find out who's helping her."

"Who?"

"Her father…"

"He's dead…"

"True, but it's him. No doubt."

Clive fell back in his seat. *Is he shitting me?* "Explain." *And it better be believable!*

Hopkins hesitated before he told the story about how he came across the man in the woods. "Here I am talking away, and the guy kept asking me why we were after his daughter."

"Stepfather, maybe?"

"No Sir. I couldn't see the guy, because of the tall brush. I asked him to step out and he said, I'm standing right beside you. Of course, I, in so many words, called him a liar. That's when he started poking me in the chest as he said, can you feel that! I did feel it, it wasn't a hard poke, but I felt it. When he grabbed my arm, I swear to you, if he hadn't let go, I would have frozen to death right where I stood. Sir, I've never felt cold like that…ever! It was like I was being grab by dry ice!"

Clive didn't know what to say. However, one question popped into his mind. "Are you telling me that you can talk to ghosts?"

"I guess I can. Never happened before, at least not that I know of. Kind of spooky."

"Interesting, thanks Hopkins. I've got to think about this."

"You and me both., sir."

"I'll bet so. Hopkins…stay close."

"Yes sir." Hopkins hung up.

Well, well, well, I wasn't expecting this! The problem that I have is, what can I do with this information? It's not like I can capture a ghost, or can I? If I get ahold of the girl, I get him too! Sounds easy, but it hasn't been. Naw, the dad doesn't matter, mainly because he can't hurt me. So where are they? It's been a week and how is she surviving?

***

Garrett watched over Megan while she bathed, her tiny body was becoming frail, she looked anemic. Now she's washed her hair and trying to comb through the tangled mess.

"Megan, how would you feel if we cut off your hair?"

"It's only tangly cause I don't have my spray, that's all."

"I mean while we're out here with no home, I think it would be easier to have short hair. Meg, it will grow back."

She didn't answer. She just continued to put on her socks and shoes. When she was finished, she picked up her 'go' bag and said, "I have to find more berries, I'm hungry."

They walked for most of the morning looking for Wapato taproots, wild carrots, and wild berries. The picking was sparse so late in the season, but she did manage to get three days' worth in her nap sack.

She sat down on a log and pouted.

"Are your gonna tell me what you're so mad about?"

After a long while she said, "I don't understand, why are we running?"

This was a conversation I really did not want to have. How do you explain to a ten-year-old that she's being hunted like an animal! The worst part is, I don't even know why. Somehow, I've got to find the answers. That guy I came across in the woods, he would know! Until I can find him, I've got to say something.

"Megan, I don't know why, I just know that they are people looking for you. Do you know if something happened recently?"

"Well, last week, mom said we had to go to the hospital, but I had to wait in the hall. This girl was on a table with wheels. They put her in the room right next to me. She looked awfully sick. All I did was go in and hold her hand for a few minutes and everyone started screaming. Mom came out and we left."

"What were they yelling?"

"They kept saying, it's a miracle! It's a miracle! One lady was crying so hard she fell on the floor. Mom thought I hurt her in some way, but I didn't daddy, I swear!"

"I'm sure you didn't…honey, miracle means good, not bad."

"Daddy, there was so much screaming. I must have done something wrong…."

"No, no, no, baby. Tell me what the little girl looked like when you first saw her."

"Well. She was white as a ghost and she was very still, she didn't cry when they tried to make her go to a new bed. There was a big fuss for a while. All kinds of people were all around her bed. And then a lady just started crying. So, they all walked away. I went over to her and touched her hand; it was very, very cold. She was all alone, daddy…so I held her hand until it got warm again."

"Then what happened?"

Megan's eyes grew wide and so serious as she spoke in a hush voice, "All of a sudden, bells and buzzers started ringing. People ran in, shoved me away, and started fussing' over her again. Mom came in and grabbed my hand; we ran."

Could it be? No, it couldn't be true! What if it was though? Could she have brought that girl back to life? And that's why they're hunting for her. I must admit, she did save Loki. I saw his miraculous recovery with my own eyes and I'm positive he was close to death.

"Then what happened?"

Megan began to cry. "When we got home, mommy told me that you had died."

"It's okay baby…."

She screamed, "No it's not! I want to go home!"

Garrett stood up. Why can't she? I'm sure they've given up on the house by now! We must be careful. "Megan…let's try."

"You mean it?"

"Yes, but we will have to sneak in and no lights at night except in your playhouse. And, you will have to sleep in your secret room. I can't say how long we'll be able to stay. So, don't cry when I tell you we have to leave, okay?"

"Okay. Let's go, please. Right now!"

"Okay…."

They stopped several times, over the next few hours, so Megan could rest and eat. Garrett had noticed when they left the den area,

Loki was following them. Garrett was grateful in case someone tried to take Megan.

"Come on Loki," called Megan. "You need to rest too."

You two rest. I'm going ahead to make sure it's safe. I'll come back and get you, okay?

"Okay."

Chapter Three
Hope

In an Amish village, called Hamlet, north of Pittsburgh, tucked back in the woods and totally secluded except for an old logging road. Nine women headed out of the village to pick wild berries along the road.

Loki and Megan had laid down to take a nap while Garret was gone. The two of them slept for about an hour or so, behind a clump of tall brushes. When they woke up, Megan heard soft footsteps, like a woman's shoe, not boots. Megan peeked out in time to see several women carrying berry baskets. Their baskets were empty, so they were just starting their gathering. Loki was starting to snarl; Megan patted his head to calm him.

What Megan didn't notice was the straggler, a young woman barely out of her teens, who saw Megan peek out to watch the others go pass. She froze in her tracks not wanting to frighten the child. *What in the world is this child doing out here? Surely, she can't be out here by herself! I really don't want to frighten her. So I will just sit down right where I am and see if she notices me.*

It wasn't long before the women left the area and Megan stepped out of the brush onto the path. She looked in the direction of the women then turned to go in the other direction. Megan stiffened and began to cry.

"I won't hurt you; I promise..."

"You'll turn me over to the bad guys!"

"Bad guys are after you?"

Megan nodded through her tears.

"I'm sorry about that, but I don't know any bad guys. My name is Hope, what's yours?"

"I can't tell you. I have to go."

Megan turned and ran into the brush.

"Don't go, you look hungry. How about you come to my house to eat some cold cuts on fresh bread. You can tell me about these bad guys."

Megan stopped running. *Food did sound good. I'm really, really hungry.* She walked back to the lady.

"I am hungry, but no bad guys."

"I swear, I live alone. No bad guys."

"Okay, um Loki comes too."

Oh my! A very large wolf stepped out of bushes to stand beside the girl. Hope swallowed hard. Do I run? That wolf can outrun me in a few feet and the girl trusts him. "Sure, I might have a few scraps for him."

Hope took Megan's hand and they went back down the path. It was only a few minutes more when Hope stopped. She said, "This is my house. I know it's small, but I call it home. So, are we good?"

Megan nodded. They went through the gate, and she opened the front door. Hope sat her at the kitchen table while she put her basket away and grabbed cold cuts out of the fridge. *This poor child is starving!*

"Excuse me, Hope. Can I go to the bathroom?"

"Of course, you can. It's just down the hall on the right. There's soap and a washcloth too."

"Thank you."

Hope rolled out enough dough to make three burritos. Hopefully it was enough. And if not, she could always make more. As she rolled the dough, she wondered how in the world this small child would end up in the woods all by herself with a wolf no less! Megan was beautiful and Hope had never seen a person with this coloring before. Her hair was jet=black, her skin was the lightest brown and those violet of hers looked right through you. She almost looked like a small gypsy, like she'd seen in history books.

The tortillas were heated, the story of how she got stranded in the woods would have to wait. In the meantime, food first. She poured a glass of milk when Megan came out of the bathroom.

She sat down at the table. Her face was rosy, pink from scrubbing and Hope could tell she felt better.

"My, my, you look pretty."

"Thank you, ma'am and I feel better too. The soap smelled so good."

"That's lavender soap! I make it myself."

"You do?"

"Yes, look out the window. See the purple flowers? That's lavender…"

"Pretty…"

"Lunch is ready…um, what is your name?"

"Megan Hollis.…"

"Pretty name.…"

Hope put the tortillas on the cutting board and began filling them with meats and cheese. In Loki's she put leftover hamburger meat. She rolled them up and set them on the table.

"How long has it been since you ate food?" Megan shrugged. "I'm going to cut them in half. You eat slowly otherwise you'll get sick, okay?"

"Yes…"

"What is his name?"

"Loki, he's a very good wolf. He says you are a friend."

"Thank you, Loki…and here is your lunch. Can you tell him not to gobble he could choke."

"He says he knows and thank you."

Hope knew there was something special about this child. She wasn't sure what it was, but she just knew that she was different. Maybe when she hears the story, she will find out.

"Loki talks to you?"

"Yes," she replied with a mouthful of food. "I'm not supposed to talk while I'm eating."

"Okay…"

They ate in silence. However, halfway through the burrito Megan ran for the bathroom. Hope got up and ran after her. The poor child was retching so hard she could barely breathe.

Hope held her under her arms. "I've got you, don't worry."

When Megan was through, she was exhausted. "How about a warm bath? I have a big shirt you can wear when you get out. Sound good?"

Megan could only nod.

Hope set her up on the toilet and began running the water. *This poor, poor child!* Tears welled up in her eyes and she just let them fall. When the tub filled, she was able to shift her focus to Megan. She took off her shoes, socks, filthy dress, and underwear vowing to burn them later. Then changed her mind, she had nothing to change her into. *Okay then, I'll scrub them and maybe I can go into the next village and buy more.*

"No need, I have clean clothes in my 'go' bag."

Was I talking out loud?

"No, I can hear your thoughts."

She had heard of people who had special abilities. "I'm going to put you in the tub first, then I'll get your 'go' bag. Can you wash yourself? If not, I'll do it for you."

"I'll try. I don't feel good."

"I know. How about you soak while I get your bag?"

Megan nodded.

"I'll be right back." She ran to the kitchen, grabbed the backpack, and ran back. "I'm going to wash you now."

Megan closed her eyes, letting the warm water soothe her. The lavender fragrance calmed her fears.

As she scrubbed the frail body, Hope couldn't help noticing all the hair gathered in her crevices.

"I was living at Loki's house. They don't have brooms."

"I suppose not." Hope couldn't help but smile. "Did you like living at Loki's?"

"There were lots of wolves…and yes, I liked it. They are my friends."

"I see, very good friends to have. Turn around please, I'm going to wash your hair."

"It's all tangly. I couldn't get my comb through it this morning."

"Okay, let me see what I can do. I'll be right back." Again, she ran to the kitchen, grabbed a bottle of olive oil and returned. Pouring a teaspoon into the palm of her hand then rubbing them together, she worked the oil into her hair. "Here you wash your bottom while your hair absorbs the oil."

Hope pulled the privacy curtain and opened the backpack. All the clothing had hair, dirt and crumpled beyond recognition. She grabbed the comb and went to her bedroom to get a pajama top, *this will do*.

When she returned, Megan was sound asleep. She ran the water, and scrubbed her hair, hoping the oil untangled the mess. Draining the water, Hope began drying her gently and pulled her out of the tub to dry her backside. She dressed her then took her to the spare room. She covered her with her granny's handmade quilt. Satisfied that she had done all she could to help the girl for now, turned to leave. Loki was standing in the doorway.

"Okay, let me get a blanket. But do not get in bed until you have a bath. Understood?"

Loki whimpered.

"I'll take that as a yes. I know you'll look after her, so if she wakes up, come, and get me."

With them both settled, Hope sat down at the kitchen table and automatically started preparing the vegetables she laid out this morning. She even put in Megan's roots. *This will make good broth; I don't think she can eat solid food yet. I have a million questions that need answers. I just have to wait until she wakes.*

In a matter of ten minutes, Loki came out of the bedroom and went to the door.

"Okay boy. Let me know when you want back in."

***

As Garrett neared the property line, he smelled smoke. He floated up until he cleared the tops of the trees. No, no......! The house was fully engulfed in flames! Those bastards, they will pay for this! How do I tell Megan she has no home to go to…dammit! *She is going to be devastated. He cussed the whole way* to where he left her, she was gone!

"Megan! Megan! Call out if you can hear me!" No response…!

No, not again. I have no idea which way she went. Although, I see footprints in the dirt, and they look like women's shoes. No little girls shoe prints though. I'll follow these and see where they lead. For hours, he tracked the footsteps. It appears that they were looking for berries. He went through every house where a set of footprints left the trail. She wasn't in any of them. So now what?

He was devastated, thinking that someone could have found her and took her to the authorities or maybe, that doctor guy got her. *Maybe someone just found her and took her home. All these options are feasible. I'll wait here for a while in case she comes back.*

* * *

The kitchen was filled with the aroma of baking bread, Hope caught herself humming. She made a couple of individual berry pies made from the berries in Megan's knapsack. It had been a very long time since she felt happy enough to hum. *Interesting,* she thought. *I do feel happy!*

Every so often, she would peek in and check on her. The poor child was sound asleep. I'll have to wake her up when dinner is ready. Hopefully she can eat a little, at least. drink some broth and keep it down.

"I like broth," a small voice said behind her.

"You're awake! Do you feel better?"

"Yes, a little bit."

"I want you to try and drink some broth. Will you do that for me?"

Megan nodded.

"If you can keep the broth down, I have sweet tarts made from your berries! Are you ready?"

"I have to wash my hands first."

"Sure, go ahead." Such a good-mannered child. She must belong to someone somewhere.

While Megan went to the bathroom, she set the table. A chunk of bread with butter and a piping hot mug of broth. Hope scooped the vegetables into her bowl and sat down.

When Megan returned. Hope said, "Just small sips, okay?"

"Can I have bread and butter first? It sure smells good!"

"Okay, if you're sure." Megan nodded. "Small bites and chew it really good."

She picked up the bread and took a bite. She chewed so long, Hope started to smile. Finally, she swallowed. Hope waited for the bolt to the bathroom, but it didn't happen.

"That's a good sign!"

Megan nodded.

"Okay, now try some broth. And you can go back and forth. We'll see how that works."

Megan did as she was told. All the food stayed down, although she couldn't eat very much because she was full.

"You did better than I thought you would!"

"I was hungry. The soup and bread were very good, thank you."

"You're most welcome, young lady. How about that tart?"

"No room maybe later."

"Sure…uh Megan where are your parents?"

"They died."

"Who takes care of you?"

"Loki and…"

"And….?"

"My dad, but now he is a ghost."

"Ghost! You said ghost…is that right?

"Yes, that's right. When my mom died last week. He came back to me, and he's been helping me ever since."

"Okay, so where is he?"

"I really don't know. He went to look at our old house to see if we could go back there. Because we've been on the run from some really bad guys that are trying to kidnap me. And that's when you found me. Where is Loki?"

"He came out of the bedroom and wanted to be let outside. And that's the last I've seen of him."

"He probably went to find my dad. To bring him here."

"Who are these bad people that are looking for you?

"I don't know. I do know they killed my mom. And then they came into the house looking for me. But I was in my playroom in the hidden room. So, they didn't find me."

"Hidden room?"

"My dad built me a playroom. There's a secret panel where I go into if anybody comes into the house. I can hide there. And no one will find me. My dad said I looked horrible, and we needed to go back there, so I could get cleaned up and stuff.

"So, you're saying. That Loki is looking for your dad and they're gonna come back here!"

"I would think so. You would like my dad. He's a real nice guy. But he got killed too. And I don't know if it's these men that killed him."

"I see."

Tears spilled down her cheeks, "I'm really tired again. Can I go lay down?"

"Of course, you can. Come on, I'll tuck you in."

Hope walked out of the bedroom and into the kitchen. *Oh my, a ghost and badmen. I wonder if any of it's true. It can't be true, can it?*

***

Garrett paced up and down the path trying to figure out what to do next. *Wait*, he stopped, *where is Loki? He must be around here somewhere.*

"Loki…come here, boy. Loki!" No response from the wolf. "I can't imagine that someone would take Megan *and* Loki…So…where are they? I can't go rummaging through every house. Or can I?"

"I wouldn't do that if I were you. Someone might take offense!"

Garrett turned around and came face to face with the officer that ran from him several days ago.

Garrett moved away from him before he spoke, "You're back…interesting. Why?"

"Looking for you…"

"Why?"

"Simple, find you, find your daughter."

"Well good luck. I have no idea where she is."

"So, I gather. Anything I can do to help?"

"Do you think I've lost my mind? Why would I let you help me? You want to take my daughter and use her as a guinea pig."

"The doctor wants to study her is all. She can do things that normal people can't do, and he wants to know how she does it."

"No…he wants to use her, and I can't let that happen. By the way, what's your name?"

"Garrett, …"

Garrett suddenly decided that he no longer wanted to talk to him. So, he just backed up about ten feet. "Well Hopkins I've got to go."

"Hey, come back. Look my boss will have my head if I don't bring back any information."

Garrett also had another thought; I can follow this guy back to his boss and find out what's going on.

Hopkins finally gave up and headed back through the woods, cussing until he got into a dark blue SUV. Fifteen minutes later he parked in front of a building, the Jenkins Institute. Garrett got out with Hopkins and followed him into a building.

Hopkins stopped at an office door that said, CEO. Hopkins knocked and heard 'enter'. He hesitated, took a deep breath, and opened the door.

"Well, Hopkins, did you find him?"

"I did, but the only thing is, he had lost her and has no idea where she is now."

"Are you serious?"

"Yes. When I first heard him, he was calling her name. And then someone named Loki. I asked him if I could help look for her. But he shot me down."

"Yeah, I suppose he did but at least you tried. Where did you find him?"

"Over by Sorensen woods…"

"There isn't anything out there, but wildlife and that old farmer, Claud something."

"Easton, I saw him in town yesterday, looked like he had a truck load of vegetables."

"That's right! The farmer's market is tonight…how about a little recon?"

"Sure… she'll be disguised if they bring her at all, you can count on it."

"Probably…let's go."

For several hours, they walked around the market even making a few purchases. However, no Megan. they returned to Jenkins' office.

"Okay…"

Hopkins left and Garrett just stared at Jenkins. *This is the guy who burnt down my house and killed my Natalie! Now this scumbag wants to capture my baby so he can study her. What kind of creep goes after children? Even if they have abilities that no one else has, you don't lock them up because they're different!*

Garrett was furious that he started a small whirl wind which lifted a stack of paperwork high into the air. The madder he got, the faster he spun and when he stopped papers and photo frames were flying up to the ceiling. And Jenkins, well, he was clearly terrified. *Good*, he thought. *That will teach him to never mess with me or Megan again.*

* * *

Hope got up before dawn to wash Megan's clothes and get them hung on the line to dry. *I wish I had money to buy her new. I don't have money for that but maybe I have enough to get a few pieces of used kids clothing from the store. Or I'll ask Grace next door if she has hand-me-downs, she has two girls.* Hope finished hanging the clothes and went inside. She found Megan sitting at the table drinking a cup of water.

"I hope you don't mind. I got a drink of water…"

"Not at all! You can get water whenever you want."

"Thank you…"

"You're welcome. I washed your clothes; they'll be dry as soon as the sun comes up."

There was scratching at the door. Megan hopped up and ran for the door, "Loki, Loki…" Megan stopped short of the door. "Can Loki come in?"

"Yes, but he gets a bath before he gets on the bed."

"Okay, thank you." Megan opened the door and flung her arms around the wolf's neck. She talked to the wolf for a while on the stoop and when she got to the part about the bath, the wolf whimpered.

Hope watched Megan interact with Loki from the kitchen window. She could see the love between them; it was palpable.

When their conversation ended, Megan and Loki came inside. It was then an extraordinary thing happened, Loki went over to Hope and laid his head in her lap. She took the wolf's face in her hands and said, "You are a good friend to Megan, and I thank you."

Loki whimpered. "He says, you good human."

Hope was truly touched in such a way that brought tears to her eyes. "Thank you…"

"Excuse me, is there a horse nearby?"

"I have a horse in the barn."

"Take me to him…hurry. Come on Loki, I need you."

She led them out the back door and Loki bolted just as the horse screamed and kicked at the walls of his stall. Next thing they heard was Loki tearing into something. Both Hope and Megan stopped when they heard the snarl of a big cat.

"Oh no, Jack!" screamed Hope.

"He's fine...Loki chased the big cat away for now. I think Loki's hurt! I can't feel him." Megan bolted for the barn. "Loki...Loki..." she ran inside the barn an found Loki laying on the floor with a deep gash in his side. "No...no..." she screamed.

Hope knelt and immediately got back up. She ran for the house and returned moments later with a rifle and towels. She pressed the towel over the wound to stop the bleeding and felt no pulse beneath her hands. She looked over at Megan who was crying and had buried her face in the wolf's neck.

"I am so sorry, Megan..."

Megan didn't acknowledge her. She was chanting something Hope couldn't understand.

That poor child. She thought. Her wolf is dead.

It took several minutes, but Loki opened his eyes and sat up.

Hope was speechless. Megan looked at her and said, "I fixed him!"

"I see that. Even his gash is healed!

"Let me look at your horse." She walked all around Jack and except for a deep cut on his behind, he was okay. Megan laid her hand on the horse's side and within seconds his gash was healed.

"Loki got here just in time. The big cat was about to land on top of your horse. Loki knocked him back. That's how he got hurt."

The stunned Hope could only mutter, "Thank you..."

Loki got up and walked outside the barn. He let out an ear-piercing howl.

"What did he just do?"

"He's calling the pack to come here to protect us."

"Why is he sitting out there?"

"He's waiting for them to talk back to him."

Loki let out another howl. This time there was a response. He took off running.

"He wants to know if they can sleep in the barn."

Hope only nodded. "I've got to feed the chickens. You should go into the house and make yourself some bread and honey. I'll be right there."

Megan seems to be unaffected by all the chaos that just happened. How is that possible? I'm a wreck! Hope filled the bucket with chicken feed and went into the chicken coop.

A bell could be heard ringing in the square. Megan came flying out of the house to see what the matter was.

"No worries, Megan. It's just the bell at the town square. If you'll be alright, I've got to go and see what the message is for today. I'll be right back."

"Okay," she replied. "Can I go in with the chickens?"

"Sure, but don't stay long."

It appears that others, in the village, saw the big cat around their chicken coops too.

"Listen," Jacob said. "If this cat is hungry enough, he will graduate to livestock. Keep your guns handy and if you can get a shot, take it. That's all."

Hope ran toward home to make sure Megan was safe. But as she rounded the barn she froze. Megan was sitting on the ground with the big cat, petting him. *What do I do?*

"Nothing," said Megan. "He won't hurt you. And he's sorry about hurting Jack and Loki, too. He was hungry is all."

"Has he eaten?"

"Yes, field rabbits. You can come and pet him."

Hope walked over and sat down by Megan. "You sure have a way with animals."

"What's that mean?"

"Well, they like you more than most folks and you can understand them where I can't."

"Sure, you can! You just have to listen harder."

"Can you help me to understand?"

Megan thought for a minute. "It's like Cumba here, see all his scars?"

Hope had not noticed them, but now she saw he was covered with them. She nodded.

"Well, a very bad man beat him every day to get him to do stuff."

"You mean like in a circus. Jump through hoops and fire?"

"He says yes. So, he ran away."

"I see, but how did you find that out?"

"Put your hand on him and close your eyes."

She reached out and laid her hand on his back.

"Cumba let Hope feel what happened to you."

Cumba laid his head in Megan's lap and closed his eyes.

Tears trickled down Hope's face. "It's like I'm there with him. I can feel his pain." The pain was too great, so she removed her hand. "I'm so sorry Cumba."

"See you can do it!"

"Can everyone do this?"

"Yes, they can. It's just that most are afraid."

"How did you know you could pet him?"

"He decides whether I'm a friend or foe. If I'm a friend, he will come to me. I don't have to do nothing…"

Hope felt the need to tell her about the meeting in the square. "Megan, he needs to leave this area. The farmers are hunting him. That's what the bell was to warn us about him. They're going to shoot him on sight!"

Megan began to cry, "Just like me…"

"No, see you are a child, and no one shoots children. But he is a lion…!"

Tug…!

"Daddy! You found me!"

Yes, Loki led me here. Loki says the farmers are hunting him. I'll be right back, I hear something.

Megan asked, "What is it daddy?"

Hope took her focus off Cumba to look at Megan. "What did you say, Megan?"

"My dad says he hears something. Maybe Cumba and Loki should hide. Loki take Cumba out to the woods, hurry."

They ran out of the yard and out of sight. Good thing too, as a group of farmers came up the road and stopped when they saw Hope feeding the chickens. Megan had run into the house and was watching from behind the sheer curtains.

"Still no sight of that lion?" asked Jacob.

"No. I certainly wouldn't be out here if I had." She held up her rifle, "I'm covered."

"Don't be out here too long."

"I won't…"

Megan, if you can hear me, stay in the house. They'll be coming back this way in a few minutes.

Hope continued feeding the animals. Once she finished, she went inside.

"Megan I'm really confused."

Megan looked up from her plate of butter bread. "What about?"

"Did I understand you correctly. Your dad is here?"

"Yes, Loki found him."

"Is he here right now?"

"No, he said he heard something and left. Now that he knows where I am, he'll be back."

"I see." Hope poured her a glass of milk and set it down in front of her. "Um, does all of this upset you?"

Megan face said it all. This child, as brave as she pretends to be, is traumatized by her mother's death, her father's return and going from living in a nice warm house to living with the wolves.

"Yes, I'm upset, and I know that cause my tummy to hurt, but I'm not afraid."

Knock, knock!

"Hide," said Hope. She watched Megan until she was clear of the room and opened the door.

A handsome young man stood there obviously nervous. He had long black curly hair tied in a ponytail and the biggest blue eyes she'd ever seen.

Hope asked shyly, "Can I help you?"

"Yes Ma'am, I'm Jeff Olsen. I'm looking for a lion named Cumba. Might you know where he is? Or have you seen him?"

"What makes you think I'd know where he is?"

"Footprints, they are all over here and he'd be hard to miss."

"Smart man."

"Well, do you know anything about him?"

"It depends...."

He frowned, "On what?"

"What are you going to do with him?"

"I built a house up in the mountains about fifty miles from here. I want to get him as far away as I can. He's a good boy and means no one any harm."

"He attacked my horse…"

"Oh, ma'am I'm so sorry, he must be hungry. I've got to find him."

"Come in and sit a bit. You looked parched."

"Yes ma'am, I am. But I must find him before he hurts someone else's livestock. They will kill him!"

It was clear to Hope that this poor man was very upset about this lion. But she needed one more piece of evidence before she brought the lion back here. "Megan, will you come out here, please?"

Megan came out of the bedroom and stood beside Hope. "Is he telling the truth?"

"Yes, he is. He really cares for Cumba. The bad man is looking for him too!"

"Okay then call Loki and have him bring Cumba back. But tell him to be careful!"

They only waited for what seemed like seconds before Loki came to the door and scratched. Hope opens the door and let in the wolf and the lion.

Jeff fell to his knees in front of the lion. He threw his arms around his neck and began to cry. "I didn't think I would ever find you. Why did you run away?"

Megan put her hand on Jeff's shoulder and said, "He was so hungry."

"I had food for him and when I turned around, he was gone."

"He says he saw the open door, so he ran."

"I left the door open for him."

"He knows…"

Jeff looked up. "You can hear him, can't you?"

"Yes…"

"We better get going. I don't want the locals to find him."

Hope handed Jeff a glass of water, before she asked, "How do we find you if we wanted to visit him. If that's okay?"

Jeff smiled and didn't try to hide his pleasure. "You are welcome anytime. I work at the zoo near Flatbush, so I can pick you both up on the way home. Do you have paper and pencil?"

Hope handed him a tablet and a charcoal pencil.

Jeff drew a map to his house and his phone number. "Thank you both so much for protecting him and for the water."

"You better get going…," said Hope taking the empty glass from him. "And feel free to stop by here anytime you're parched or hungry."

Jeff tipped his hat and in a split second they were gone. Hope waved as the truck drove past. How she missed Paul, her husband. He fell from the loft and broke his neck last year. *Now I'm all alone.* How she longed for someone to hold her and feel another's warmth against her body. Seeing this extremely handsome man brought up all these intimate feelings she thought she buried with her husband.

Chapter Four
The Search

Clive screamed and instantly sat up in bed. He was dripping in sweat accompanied by a pounding headache. It's the same nightmare over and over. *When will it end? All I remember is, I couldn't save him. Enough of this, I'm going to the office, Hopkins is due to meet me there soon. Maybe then I can shake these feelings, at least for a little while.*

The office door had new glass and he hoped the inside was cleaned up too. *If Hopkins is to be believed, I had a visit from Megan's father. I've never been so frightened in my life.* The office was cleaned up and all the paperwork put in a neat stack on his desk. The carpets vacuumed and the shelves cleaned and polished. He sat down but got a creepy feeling like he was being watched. Paranoia!

Hopkins arrived on time, and he brought breakfast. "You look awful, bad night?"

"Yeah, something like that. Let's eat and then we can drive around for a while."

"Sure…"

They drove the back roads for what seemed like hours and found nothing.

Hopkins asked, "Why did you start the institute?"

Jenkins was quiet for a short while, "My brother, mainly…"

Hopkins stayed silent.

"Matt died when he was twelve years old…"

"I'm sorry, Clive…"

"Thanks, but he was frail and sick in bed most of his life. But one night when he was seven, I heard him talking to someone in the middle of the night. I crossed the hall and peeked into his room. He was deep in conversation, however there was no one else in his room. Night after night the conversations continue. So, one morning, at breakfast, I asked him who he was talking to. He said a lot of people come to talk to him. Of course, I didn't believe him. So, I hid in his room to witness these conversations for myself. I made a bed in his closet and covered it up with a quilt. I must have fallen asleep because the next thing I know Matt is talking to someone. I looked out at the louvered slates in the closet door. In the moonlight that was streaming through the window, and I saw a person standing by my brother's bed. I couldn't hear what the guy was saying. So, I moved closer to get a better look! Jerry, I could see right through the guy!"

"That can't be all there is?"

"Well, no. It's what happened the day he died."

"What happened?"

"I told you he was sickly and by the time he was eleven, he never left his bed. It was his twelfth birthday; the doctor came to the house to check him over. When he came out of his room, he informed us that he only had a few hours to live. We all went in to sit with him until the end. When it became apparent, he was at the end, we all put our hands on him. Mom told him it was okay to go to heaven. Within seconds, we all saw what looked like smoke coming out of his chest. Everyone jumped back to watch what was happening. The smoke went up to the ceiling and hovered there for a minute or two. I swear I saw my brother wave goodbye."

"Amazing…so the institute is in honor of your brother?"

"More like because of him."

"I get it …you want to know what happens after death."

"Sort of, I want to know why some people have the gift like the girl. I saw her bring a dead girl back to life! Combine that with my brother talking to ghosts and his ascension, brought me to the conclusion that there are things happening in this world that we don't understand."

"I see what you mean…" Jerry sat back in his seat to ponder all that Clive told him. I don't know why I could hear the dad either. I've never experienced anything like that before ever.

"We've been at this for hours. Let's eat. There's a diner over by Junction 14."

"Sounds perfect, I'm hungry."

Fifteen minutes later, they pulled into the parking lot of Lilly's Diner.

Jerry hopped out of the truck. "I don't think I've ever been here. Is the food good?"

Clive smiled, "The best home cooking around."

As they walked inside, a perky young woman hollered out, "Clive! Long time no see…"

"It's been a while, lots of work. Two coffees please."

"Sure thing, be right there."

She brought menus and coffee. "I'll be back to take your order."

"Thanks Mary…"

"I could eat a horse," said Jerry as he studied the menu looking for a large sandwich or dinner.

Clive didn't respond; he was reading a newspaper that someone left in the booth. "Hey Jerry, listen to this! A man was walking by Flatbottom lake and saw a small girl on the other side washing her face. What struck him odd was that there were no adults watching out for her. Suddenly, there was a pack of wolves around her urging her to leave. He swears one of the wolves looked straight at him and in an instant, they were gone. He drove around to where he saw them and there was no trace of them at all. No footprints, nothing."

Mary returned and took their orders.

Hopkins chuckled, "Flatbottom is hardly bigger than a pond…"

"Yeah, I know. So where did they go?"

"Only one place I can think of; there's a den nearby!"

In a few minutes, Mary brought their sandwiches and noticed Clive reading the newspaper. He was focused on an article on the front page. "I hear-tell several people have seen her lately and always around the lake. Enjoy gentlemen."

"Thanks," said Jerry with a mouthful. "We will."

Neither of them spoke until they were halfway through their meals. "You know Clive, finding that den will be near impossible."

"So, I've been told. But there must be some signs…"

"No way to know unless we look…"

Clive paid the bill and they climbed into the truck heading for Flatbottom Lake.

"We don't know where he was when he spotted the girl, right?"

"The article didn't say, but my guess would be the farthest point away from people."

The Flatbottom Lake sign came into view and Clive prepared to make the left turn onto a road that was clearly washed out.

"Hang on…this is going to be a bumpy ride."

Ruts and deep potholes tossed the men around the cab like pretzel sticks. When they came to a stop, the lake was stunningly blue. Five picnic tables flanked the water's edge which made the scene more picturesque!

"This is not what I remember as a kid…," whispered Clive not wanting to break the spell.

"I've never been here but you can bet I'll be back! Damn, it's beautiful here." Hopkins opened his door and slid out.

Clive did the same. They both walked over to a table and sat on top of it, their feet resting on the bench seat. Across the lake were mature walnut trees and berry bushes. But the most startling sight was the grapevines that traversed the tree trunks nearly up to the canopy.

"I think a ladder would be awesome about now." Hopkins pointed. "Look at those grapes! There must be hundreds of bunches!"

"We could make a killing at the farmers market tonight."

"Oh yeah, I think so," informed Hopkins. "It just so happens I have a ladder in the back and trash bags, the big heavy-duty ones!"

"Seriously? "Clive asked. "Then let's go!"

It took a while to drive around to that part of the lake, the ruts were horrible. They hopped out, grabbed the equipment, and went looking for paw prints or a child's. By the time they finished getting a dozen big bags of grapes, dusk was rapidly approaching. If they were going to sell the grapes, they better get going. They decided to pack up when they heard….

Grrrr…

Clive could feel the wolf's breath on the back of his thigh. He swallowed hard and dared not to move. He looked across the bed of the truck at the terror-stricken face of Hopkins. His eyes kept going down and to the left. Clive nodded slightly.

Grrrr…

This time the wolf's teeth were against Clive's inner thigh, the most tender part of the leg. One false move and the wolf will rip his leg to shreds. Sweat beads were forming on both their faces. But Hopkins was turning red and looked like he was going to pass out.

Clive whispered, "Jump up and into the truck, hurry."

Hopkins shook his head, no…

Well, he wasn't about to be a wolf's dinner, so he took a deep breath and leapt. The wolf grabbed his leg tearing flesh and muscles. Clive pulled his gun out of his waistband and shot the wolf dead. The rest of the wolf pack ran off, but one wolf turned and stared at him for a few seconds, then he left.

Hopkins ran around the truck and knelt beside Clive. Hopkins took off his belt a made a tourniquet for the leg that was bleeding profusely.

"This is bad. I'm going to get you into the truck and drive you to the hospital."

Clive could only nod and once he was safe inside the truck, he passed out.

Hopkins drove like a mad man and notified the hospital he was on his way.

The truck tires screeched as he slid to a stop in the ambulance bay and laid on the horn. Medical personal rushed out with a gurney, gently pulled Clive out and it only took a second for the doctor to yell, "Surgery stat!"

Hopkins went to follow them, but his legs gave way and he fell to the pavement.

Chapter Five
Horace Hamilton

Hope decided not to get the hand-me-downs and bought cloth at the General Store instead. Hand-me-downs might draw suspicion and questions which would not fare well for Megan. She pulled out her mother's old pedal sewing machine and set it up on the table. With the measurements she took off of Megan this morning, she began to cut the material. She had watched her mother make the dresses a thousand times. So, she was pretty sure that she could make something for this child to wear. Once she had all the pieces cut out, she began to sew.

"Hope," A small voice said behind her. "Am I gonna have to go to school?"

Oh my! I hadn't thought about school and with people looking for her, it's best that she stays inside as much as possible. "How about if I teach you for a while at least."

Megan's eyes lit up. "Yes, please."

"Okay, then we'll start first thing tomorrow morning."

"Thank you. What can I do till then?"

"Well, I was going to plant a vegetable garden today. How do you feel about planting?"

"I know how to plant. I used to do that with my mom sometimes."

"That's great! We'll have a great time."

"Okay, so what can I do right now?"

"Well, you could clean that bowl of vegetables over there. I'm goanna make something special tonight and those vegetables would be really good with my meal."

"Sure, I can do that."

Hope continued with her sewing. She couldn't believe how happy she was. The Wolves were back in their den, and no one had come looking for Megan. Suddenly, there was a scratch at the door.

And Megan ran to open it, hoping it was Loki, but it wasn't. It was Mazey! Megan backed away and let the wolf in. And she knew instantly something was horribly wrong.

What is it, Mazey? What's happened?

Those awful men killed Hazel.

Do you know where my dad is? He could help you.

No, I don't. And I don't know how he can help.

Hope was not privileged to hear their conversation between the Wolf and the girl, so she asked., "What's happening? What's going on?"

Megan had tears running down her face. "Somebody killed Hazel."

"Is that one of the wolves?"

"Yes."

"Can you help her?"

"Probably not now, she might have been dead, too long."

Megan turned to Mazey, "When did this happen?"

"Now... Help...."

"I don't know if I can, but I could try."

Mazey where did this happen?

Lake

Megan frowned. "That is a very long way."

Hope said. "I have a horse and buggy. Will that help?"

What do you think, Mazey?

Mazey whimpered and moved toward the door.

"Wait here until I bring the buggy around. You both will have to hide until we get past town and get into the country. Get a blanket to cover yourselves in case someone spots me, and I have to stop for a minute or two.

It seemed like it took forever to get out of town and away from the houses. Macy jumped out and ran ahead of them. When she got to Flatbottom Lake turnoff the horse reared.

Hope asked, "Are all the wolves around Hazel?"

"Probably so. We should hear them talking soon."

"That's probably what Jack hears. Okay, can you tell them not to talk until I get closer?"

"Sure, I can do that. Mazey, tell them to stop talking for a minute."

Suddenly, there was silence and Jack settled down.

Hope could see the circle of wolves; they had laid down. She got as close as she dared.

Megan, however, leapt out of the buggy and ran for Hazel. She got her on her hands and knees, running her hands across Hazel's body and felt no life. Then suddenly her eyes widened.

"Hope, Hazel's pregnant! And I think there's a puppy still alive."

"Oh my! What do we do? How do we get it out? I know! We need something sharp. Let me see what I can find." She ran to the buggy hoping to find a vegetable knife or hoof tool. Under the seat, she touched something hard and pulled it out. *A hoof tool it is!*

Megan reached out for the tool and Hope was astonished asked, "You're going to do this?"

"Yes, I know how."

All Hope could do was stand back and watch. Megan cut, with precision, about a three-inch incision. Next, she pushed the abdomen until a membrane peeked out and she carefully opened the uterus and pulled out a pup.

"Give me the pup, you check for more."

Megan pulled out all the pups, no others survived. She turned to Hope, "Boy or girl?"

"Girl and she is beautiful!"

Mako rose and walked over to Hope. He sniffed her and washed her face. *She will remember me now; we will call her Haze to honor her mother.*

"Haze is a fitting name, thank you, Mako. She needs mother's milk. Is there a wolf that can feed her?"

Not at this time.

"Hope there are no mothers that can feed her!"

"I have goats' milk, but that would mean she would come with us for five weeks. We will bring her back once she is weaned."

"Mako, do we have your permission to take her with us with the promise to return her when she is old enough?"

Mako laid down in front of Hope and Megan and looked from one face to the other. It was clear he was perplexed as to what he should do.

Hope laid Haze between his paws and said, "Mako, I promise to return her. She will die without food. She has to be able to eat on her own."

Mazey came over to him and nudged his shoulder. He hung his head in sadness. With tears in his eyes, he nuzzled Haze until the scent of her covered his face and paws. He rose and walked back to the pride; they walked off.

Megan said to Mazey, "Show Hope where the den is so we can return her…is it far?"

No…

Hope and Mazey rose and walked toward the tree line. Megan picked up the crying pup and held her next to her chest in hopes her heartbeat would quiet her; it did not.

A mother fox, hearing the puppy's cries decided to investigate. She approached Megan curiously, more interested in the pup than the human.

This baby has no mother, she lies dead over there. She is hungry, can you help her?

The fox seemed surprised that a human could talk to her. She came closer and laid down showing full teats. Megan put the puppy onto a teat, and she immediately began to suckle.

Thank you, Ms. Fox, for helping us. The puppy had fallen asleep. The fox got up slowly so as not to wake her.

I am called Jax, I never believed I could or would talk to a human. I am honored for the privilege.

"It is I who is honored."

The fox scampered to the woods, but before she disappeared, she looked back. Megan smiled and waved goodbye.

It wasn't long before Hope entered the clearing. Megan had wrapped Haze in her pinafore and nestled back against the tree.

Hope emerged from the woods. "Everything alright?"

"Yes fine. Did you see the den?"

"Yes, and I notched the trees so I can find my way back! I understand why you felt safe there. They are quite impressive your wolves."

"I don't know what that means. I just know they protected me from the bad guys. Um, Jack's thirsty, better take him to the lake."

"Thanks, I will. We have to go; it will be dark soon."

"Okay."

Megan and Haze were loaded up into the buggy, while Hope lit the lantern and hung it up on the pole to light the way.

"The puppy is awfully quiet. Shouldn't she be crying for food?"

"She already ate…"

Hope stared Megan…*no not possible!* "Uh Megan, how did the puppy get fed?"

"A momma fox, named Jax, heard Haze crying and came to help her. I asked the fox if she would feed her, and she did!"

Hope relaxed, "That's incredible! I didn't know that animals helped each other like that."

"All the time. They are no different than we are."

"Can I ask you how you knew to cut the puppy out?"

Megan was still for a while. "I just knew…"

"You said you had done this before, where?"

"I don't know where, but I was bigger…"

Megan bigger? So, she continued questioning her, "Bigger? How much bigger?"

"Big like you…"

"Like a grown up?" Megan nodded. "Do you know what kind of work you did?"

"I was a doctor…"

"That's incredible…a doctor is a noble profession."

"Noble, like a King?"

Hope chuckled, it's hard to talk to a child that acts like she's forty. "Sort of, yes."

Megan was happy with that explanation and continued her cooing to Haze. However, Hope was beyond baffled that Megan meant that she was an older person at some point, or that she was a doctor. Hope didn't know what to think. However, from what she saw today, she was pretty sure that Megan might still be connected to her past life. She had heard of children that remembered who they were before coming here, but the memory would fade about three years of age. This child is so extraordinary, she doubted that she was qualified to take care of her. The only thing she decided she could do was follow her lead and protect her.

By the time they arrived home, Haze was hungry again and letting the whole world know it. Megan ran into the house while Hope put Jack in the barn. Next, she milked a goat and came into the house.

"Megan, will you bring Haze out here please…"

Megan came running and handed the pup to Hope. "I'm a mess, I have to clean up is that okay? I won't be long, I promise."

"Take all the time you need; we will be fine."

"I don't want to burden you, I'm responsible for her."

"First, we are responsible. I made promises too. Second, this is not a burden to me. I love baby animals! This will be my first time caring for a wolf puppy, so I will need you to show me how, okay?"

Megan beamed, "Okay!"

As Megan disappeared into the bathroom, Hope continued feeding Haze. The baby wolf was bigger than most dog pups she'd seen, and her markings were stunning. She was solid black with gray feet. She grabbed a small basket from underneath the table. Next, she grabbed a handful of scrap material out of her quilting bag and made a bed in the bottom of the basket. *There*, she thought, *this looks good for now.*

"Is she sleeping?" Megan wanted to know the instant she came out of the bathroom.

Hope smiled at the dripping wet child. "Dry off, put on your night clothes, and then come look. I hope you like what I did…"

Within a minute, Megan came around the corner. She inspected the pup, the bedding and when she was finished, she said, "She needs to be washed."

Hope went to the linen shelf and got a washcloth. Warming the water on the stove, she dipped the washcloth and wrung it out. "Would you like to bathe her?"

Her eyes lit up, "Sure!"

"Okay here you go. I'll get a fresh towel."

"And a clock, if you have one."

"I think I do out in the barn. I will be right back."

The backdoor opened, Hope returned with a clock and some straw. "I remembered at the den there was straw on the floor."

"It's not straw, it's dried grasses."

"Okay…I'm betting she will sleep better if we put this underneath her bedding. What do you think?"

Megan looked at Hope with such admiration, Hope was taken off guard.

"I think it is perfect! And Haze will be happy too!"

"Great! Let's get set up for tonight. The puppy will be up a lot. Do you want to take turns feeding her throughout the night?"

"Okay, me first!"

"If you wish…I'll get the milk and syringes set up for you. It's late. Are you ready?"

"Yes…I'm tired too."

The sunlight woke Hope, and she sat up with a start! Megan and Haze…she ran to Megan's room and stopped at the door. Megan lay on her back with Haze laying on her chest. She had pulled up the quilt to cover the puppy. The scene was picture perfect! She had never known such love and a purpose for her life. She carefully removed Haze and put her in the basket. Tiptoeing out of the room, she got dressed and went to the kitchen. The sun was bright and covered the table, so she put the basket next to the window.

Suddenly, there was a knock on the door. Hope covered the basket with a dish towel before she opened the door. "Horace, can I help you?"

"Yes Ms. Langley, your two years of mourning is nearly up, and I wanted you to know the Vicker granted me permission to court you."

"He did, did he?"

"Yes…I know this is not your original village. We have different laws here so you should know according to our laws you cannot remain single and own property."

"You're saying if I don't marry, they can take my animals and property?"

"Yes, you have two choices, marry, or leave. You can take the animals you purchased, just not the ones the village gave Paul to start the farm."

"I see. Thank you for the information. Goodbye." Hope slammed the door.

Now what? I only have six months to figure this out!

Haze began squealing…Megan was standing in the hall. She didn't say anything but ran to Haze. She wet the washcloth and began stimulating the puppy over the sink so she would go to the bathroom. Hope heated more milk and filled syringes.

Megan had heard what Horace had said, although she didn't understand all of it. Megan knew it was something bad for Hope. She began to cry softly.

Hope heard her whimpering and instantly went to her. She faced her and said, "We will be okay. Do you understand?"

"It's my fault you're going to lose your house and animals…"

"This has nothing to do with you, honey. It's the laws of this village. I have a plan. We can go to my village. We will be welcomed there."

"Are you sure?"

"Yes, I'm sure. I never liked it here anyway. I was only here because this is my husband Paul's village."

"How about we take a ride tomorrow to my village? We'll pack a lunch and bring milk for Haze, we'll have fun!"

Megan frowned, "All these horrible things have happened since you took me in, it's my fault!"

"I see. So, I suppose you made that awful rule?"

"No…"

"And you asked the lion to come and attack Jack?"

"No…"

"What about Hazel getting shot? Did you shoot her?"

"No…"

Hope sat back and waited. Surely, she will realize that none of these things were her fault. Haze began to fuss so Hope picked her up and took her outside. When Hope came in, Megan was not at the table.

"Megan where are you?" No response! In fact, she was not in the house anywhere. *Oh no, I forgot she is a child. I must have been too harsh with my explanation.* She fed Haze and put her in the basket, loaded more syringes and went out to the barn. Hitching up Jack to the buggy, she took off down the road toward the wolf den. She held Jack for a walk so she could look on both sides of the road. After two hours, she turned onto the road to Flatbottom Lake. No sign of her anywhere.

She got out of the buggy. Without knowing what to do next, she did the only thing she could think of. Cupping her hands, she put them to her mouth and yelled, "Mazey! I need you! Megan is in trouble!" When several minutes had passed, she called out again and waited. She didn't have to wait long this time; the wolf pack came bounding out of the woods.

Mazey stopped in front of Hope and looked up at her. She knelt in front of Mazey, "Mazey, Megan is lost in the woods, and we must find her, please help me!"

Mazey licked her hand and took off running, but then turned back. She nudged Hope toward the buggy. "You want me to go home?" She barked, turned, and ran away.

Hope took Jack to the lake to drink enough water for the trip home. When he finished drinking, she walked him over to a patch of wild grass that grew under the trees in hopes he would eat. But he only ate a few mouthfuls. Suddenly, she heard howling! Maybe they found her!

Mazey came running toward her at full speed. She grabbed Hope's skirt in her teeth and pulled it.

"Okay girl. I'll follow you." She tied Jack to the tree loosely so he could eat if he wanted to. Grabbing the basket, she began to run behind Mazey. When Mazey stopped, Hope looked around not quite understanding and then she saw it. Men's shoe prints and a small child!

"No...no...no, they caught her!" Hope sat down on the ground and cried. Mazey whimpered. Hope looked up. "Thanks to all of you for helping. But very bad men have taken Megan and I don't know who they are." Hope stood, "Will you take me back to my horse?"

Mazey pulled her skirt and led her back to where she left the buggy. However, someone was sitting at the picnic table. Mazey growled. The man looked up; it was Jeff Olsen!

"It's okay Mazey. He is a friend. You better get going, I'll be fine."

Mazey hesitated, but with a pat on the head from Hope, she and the pack left.

"Wolves!"

"Well, yes...they are friends of Megan's. She lived with them for a short time. I think they just tolerate me. How is Cumba?"

"He's great but lonely, so I'm going to try and free another lion. I just have to pick the right time."

Of course, Haze started to squeal. Jeff's eyes widened when Hope pulled out the large wolf pup.

"My word young lady a wolf pup!"

"Yes, her mama was killed and none of the other wolfs had pups. So, Megan and I took on the job." She started to cry.

"Oh, I'm so sorry..."

"I'm not crying about the wolf. Megan's been kidnaped by extremely bad people. The same people who killed her parents and the wolf. I have no way to find her."

"Wow, you say you don't know who they are?"

"No, I never heard a name. I just know they been chasing her for a while now."

"So, she was hiding out with you?"

"Yes…"

"Why were they after her?"

"That's a much bigger story. One I don't think you'll believe." She finished feeding and expressing the pup. "Jeff, I must get going, it's a two-hour ride home. I want to be there before dark."

"Uh, want company?"

Hope looked around and realized his truck wasn't there. "I'm embarrassed, I was so caught up in my own problems that I did not notice that your truck wasn't here. What happened? Can I take you somewhere?"

"My truck broke way back down the road. So, I walked over here to wait for the tow truck to pick it up and I saw your buggy."

"You knew it was my buggy, how?"

He blushed a bit. "When I was looking for Cumba I climbed around your barn. Your buggy was there, and I looked inside to make sure he wasn't hiding. I noticed your beautiful quilt."

"I see." Now it was her turn to blush. "Thank you."

Jeff smiled, "I'd like to talk for a while. If that's ok?"

"But I live so far away, how will you get home?"

"My brother will bring me my truck when it's fixed. I'm sure it's something minor. So that leaves me time to hear your story if you're willing to tell me plus I've always wanted to go on a buggy ride."

She smirked, "You have, have you?"

"Yes ma'am…"

"Well then, it looks like Haze is full and happy, so we better get started."

Hope and Jeff chatted the whole trip like long lost friends. He was curious about Megan.

"It's obvious that you two are not related."

"True.... I found her in the woods not far from my house."

Jeff was taken back! "Found her? What does that mean, found her?"

"Well, just that. I was on my way to pick berries for my pies and there she was beside the path with a wolf protecting her."

Jeff shook his head, "Someone dumped that beautiful little girl in the woods?"

"Not exactly," Hope hesitated to tell him the whole story. "I don't know how much I can say without putting her in more danger...."

"Danger! What kind of danger can a small child be in?"

"One that can heal the dead...."

Jeff couldn't believe his ears. "Are you serious? No one can do that!"

Hope didn't say anything.

Jeff looked at Hope, "Are you sure about this?"

Hope nodded, "I've seen her do it. And, according to Megan people are trying to capture her because she has the ability. Which makes perfect sense when you think about it. Can you imagine how much money someone could make with a person like her?"

Jeff was alarmed, "They could do some real harm to get her..."

"Oh, they have already, they've killed both her parents!"

"I'll bet she ran..."

"Yes, exactly." Hope to a deep breath and said, "Her dead father is helping her!"

Jeff was sure this lady hit her head on a rock and was delusional. He felt a tug on his shirt and looked around. Another tug, and another. "What the hell!"

"Garrett, tug his shirt two times if you're here."

Tug…tug…Jeff held up both of his hands. "I surrender to the craziness!"

Hope and Jeff put the buggy and Jack away and headed to the house. By the time they got home, Hope was smitten with Jeff. He was so easy to talk to and she bore her soul. She told him about the conversation that led to Megan running away. Next was Horace's threats that she would lose her farm and the very strict rules of the village, lastly the wolves that protect her and Megan.

"All of this happened in a week?"

"Yes…I'm not used to anything but an ordinary day. Although, I have to say, I feel alive and purposeful."

"I see how all this could really change your life."

Hope heated up her homemade soup and put out a plate of fresh bread and butter. "Dig in…"

Jeff, after one bite said, "This is delicious! It's rare that I get a homemade meal and this bread is so fresh!"

"Thank you, it's nice to share a meal, I didn't realize how much I missed it." and here comes a flood of tears. "I'm sorry, I just can't stop."

"It's okay," he said reaching over to hold her hand. "What can we do to find Megan?"

"I have nowhere to start. If her dad was here and could be heard, he'd know where to look. But as it is…. I'm lost."

"So, unless we get a clue, there is nothing we can do."

"Yes…"

"What about the farm?"

"I only have a few animals that are mine. The rest stay here including Jack." Another round of tears. "I'm sorry I can't seem to hold it together."

"Don't worry please it's okay. You've been through a lot this week. I have a feeling you needed to cry."

"You may be right; I do feel a bit better. I guess I was all pent up as my momma used to say."

"Are your parents alive?"

"No. I'm alone now."

"Sorry, I definitely know how that feels…"

"You too?" He nodded. "Sorry…"

"I really thought I was okay," he explained. But I swear, it only takes one small thing to bring it all up again. It feels like I have to come up from the depths of despair again. It's a vicious circle."

"Yes, it does feel exactly like that…anyway, I thought I'd go back to my village, but now I don't feel like that's the place for me either. I'll figure it out, I've got just over seven months to decide. But first, I have to get this puppy old enough to be weaned. She needs to be with her family, so, she can learn wolf things."

"Sounds like fun."

"It is and she keeps me company at night. I didn't realize how lonely I was until I found Megan…she put such a light in my life and now…" tears welled up and Hope ran for the bathroom.

Jeff was touched by the depth of her compassion. The women he usually came across were callous and self-centered. She actually thought about another human being besides herself which was refreshing, and she endeared herself to him when he wasn't looking.

Knock, knock.

Jeff got up and opened the door. This was no doubt, Horace.

"Can I help you."

The shocked man said, "I'm here to see Hope."

"I'm sure she would like to see you. However, she is indisposed at the moment. I'll be happy to tell her you came by."

"I'll wait…" and started to come up the steps.

"I'm sorry sir, you will have to wait outside. Only family can be inside. There is a bench right there, have a seat. I'll send her out." Jeff shut the door in his face, and he wasn't the least bit sorry either. *Pompous ass!*

Jeff heard the bathroom door open. When Hope emerged, her eyes were red and swollen from crying. "I hate to tell you that Horace is sitting outside waiting for you."

"No! Did he insult you in any way?"

"Not him no…but he did try to come in and I told him only family can be inside. He wasn't happy."

"Oh my…," she giggled. "I'd better go out so he will leave."

"I see a shotgun over there…"

"You are so bad!" She winked, "Maybe next time!" She opened the door, stepped out and closed it behind her. She sat at the opposite end of the bench from Horace.

So proper, Jeff thought. What a bland relationship that would be. Doing his bidding day after day, yuck! He suddenly realized; he was jealous! It's not possible to be jealous only after meeting someone twice, is it? No not possible, he just felt sorry for her situation.

Finally, after what seemed like an eternity, she stood and walked through the front door. She leaned her back against the door, she had been crying again.

"What did that man say to you?"

"He said that no other man can ask for my hand until I come out of my mourning period, and that the Vicker approve his request to court me again."

"Are you serious? Of all the nerve…who does he think he is?"

"It's not his fault. There are rules here and he is within his rights to claim me…"

"CLAIM YOU!" he yelled. "I'm sorry, I find this whole situation apprehensible! You are not a trophy to be claimed or a prize to be won at the fair." Suddenly, he blurted, "Marry me. That way he has no claim on you."

Hope's jaw dropped and she moved to the table so she could sit down. "Jeff…you don't want to marry me! I am damaged goods."

"How do you figure that, pray tell?"

"I'm a widow and… I… can't bear children." She hung her head in shame.

"So that's not a big deal; you can adopt or foster children! None of this puts a 'claim ticket' on you! You're better than what they are trying to make you believe. Please don't let them do this to you, please. Marry me…we would have a great life. I'm not rich but I'm loyal and a good person. I have a steady income and a farm which is paid for by the way. Please think about this carefully."

Honk, Honk

Hope looked out the window and saw Jeff's truck. "Your brother is here, and I promise I will think about everything you said, now go. Haze will be waking up soon."

"Okay, I'll be here tomorrow after work."

"Okay…tomorrow."

Hope sat there in stunned silence for what seemed like hours, in truth it was probably only ten minutes. "Holy cow! What just happened?"

Chapter Six
Captured

Clive woke up in excruciating pain. "Awe damn!" He searched for a call button and pressed it.

"Mr. Jenkins, you're awake. I'll be right in with a pain shot."

"Hurry up!" He yelled through clinched teeth.

"Yes sir."

An older woman in her late fifties entered his room, shot in hand. Scrubbing his arm with an alcohol pad, she gave him the shot. "Your dinner will be up at five."

"It better not be Jello…! Heads will roll!" he yelled after her. The nurse just lifted her hand, waved, and kept walking.

"Bitch!" He tried to roll over onto his side and he screamed, "Damn that hurts."

"What hurts?" A voice said from the doorway.

"Hopkins, come in. I'll be glad to have some intelligent conversation. The only language these people speak is medicine."

"Well, I have some news to cheer you up."

"Good, I need cheering up. Ask that old nurse out there. I just bit her head off."

Jerry sat down and was grinning like a Cheshire cat. "I found her, and we have her…"

Clive sat up. "That is awesome! Where did you find her?"

"In the woods, she was just walking alongside the road. When she heard the truck, she stepped into the woods and sat down. It looks like she'd been crying."

"Did she give you any trouble?"

"Not a bit. But she's not talking. Total silence."

"So, something happened to her. I wonder what it could be."

"Don't know. So, hurry up and get out of here."

"Yes, I will. They're going to cast my leg tomorrow. That damn wolf nearly tore my leg completely off."

"You kill his mate; what did you think he would do?"

"I didn't mean to kill her. I only wanted to scare her off. So, she'd stop coming toward me.

"Well Clive, she was pregnant and, to hear the paramedics tell it, Megan saved one of the pups."

"Saved how?"

"She did a Cesarean…right there in the field."

"No way…! A ten-year-old performing surgery! Are you sure?"

"Yes…and the paramedic said, she operated on the wolf like a professional."

Clive was dumbfounded…the more he learns about her abilities, the more he has to know how she does it. "Okay, well, call me if she starts talking! Better yet record everything she says."

"I will…"

Three days later, Clive rolled into the institute in a wheelchair, under strict orders that he was not to put any weight on the leg for six weeks. He was not happy about that but if he ever wanted to walk again, he had to follow the doctor's orders to the letter.

Hopkins was walking toward him. "Where is she? Take me to her, now!"

"Easy Clive you're going to bust a stitch."

Clive wanted to slap him silly for talking to him like that, but he sat back and waited to be pushed to her room. It seemed like forever to get there. Hopkins opened the door and there sat Megan Hollis! *Oh my god! She's here!*

"Hello Megan, my name is Clive Jenkins. How are you doing?"

Silence…

"Okay, let me explain, I'm curious as to how you can heal people. I know you can, because I saw you bring that girl back to life in the hospital. I'm really interested in how you are able to do that."

Silence…

Well, he thought, this isn't working. Maybe I'll try a different approach.

"Hey Hopkins, how about finding her an ice cream sundae?" Megan turned and faced the window. "Or maybe a sandwich with fries?"

Megan don't react, it's dad. I don't want them to know I'm here, okay.

Okay, but I'm glad you are here.

Me too baby, me too. Okay, here's what we are going to do. First just stay silent. Second, don't eat what they bring you. I will bring you food.

Okay daddy. I don't like him, he killed you and mommy.

True, I'm going to bring Hope here immediately.

Oh yes please, hurry daddy!

First food, I'll be right back.

Okay…

"Look Megan, you must eat sometime. So, what do you say, a burger and fries?"

Megan didn't move or acknowledge him.

"Let's go. She can starve for all I care."

"Give her some time Clive…"

"I'm not a patient man."

Hopkins opened the door so Clive could wheel himself out. As soon as they were out of sight, a woman came in with a ham sandwich, her favorite.

"Eat child before they come back. I'll bring you more tonight. Don't get caught."

Megan nodded and turned toward the window so they couldn't see what she was doing. She ate quickly and got up to go brush her teeth. She captured all the crumbs in her pinafore so she could flush them. She definitely did not want the nice lady to get into trouble. Once all that was accomplished, she brushed her hair and sat back down.

It wasn't long before Clive returned with the kind nurse who fed her earlier. Clive was babbling about something, and she refused to listen to him.

Clive pounded the table with his fist. Megan's head snapped around to look at him. "Now that I have your attention, Missy. All I want to know is how you heal people. Where does the ability come from?"

She turned and faced the window.

He killed my parents and now he wants my secrets…no way…

Suddenly, there was a commotion out in the hall. Megan turned around and saw Hope arguing with Hopkins. Megan got up and ran around the table out of Clive's reach. She slammed open the door and ran to Hope as fast as she could. Hope scooped her up and took her out of the building. Jeff was waiting for her and the instant they climbed into his truck, he gassed it.

"Megan and Hope clung to each other like long lost people. Both were crying and apologizing because, one ran away and the other who spoke too harshly. By the time they got to Hope's house, Megan had fallen asleep. Jeff carried her in, and Hope put her to bed. When Hope came back to the kitchen, Jeff said, "You know he'll come after her again."

"Yes, I know, but what can I do?"

"I have an idea. I'm not sure you're going to like it."

She smiled, "Okay… go ahead and tell me."

"It will take at least a couple of days for Clive to find you. I'm off work tomorrow. So, why don't I come back and pick up you, Megan, and Haze. I'll take both of you to my farm. Cumba would love to have you there."

"What about the animals?"

"Ask your Vicker to get someone to feed them while you're gone on a family emergency or whatever you want to say. Look these guys are killers and make no mistake, they will come after you again. So, pack up what you can, clothes and such, all the things you'll need. What do you think?"

"Are you sure, we barely know each other and you're willing to put your life on the line to hide us."

Without hesitation, he said, "Yes…"

"Why?"

"I don't want anything to happen to either of you. And the only way I can protect you is by putting you where they can't find you. Do you understand?"

"I guess what I'm asking is why would you consider doing such a thing? Make no mistake, I am flattered. And, true this idea of yours would solve all our problems, but…"

"No buts, please accept my offer."

"I'm going out back and think a minute. I think I hear Haze waking up. There are syringes in her basket which she is rapidly out growing. I'll be back in a few minutes."

Jeff nodded and picked up Haze. "My, my, look at how much you've grown!"

Hope sat down on the stoop not sure what to do. She really liked Jeff, but things were just moving too fast. It's true she needed an instant solution to her problems however, she wasn't sure this was the right way to go. And she was quite sure that she would be grateful to get out of this village. Too many rules and regulations, too much of everything. Why does everything have to be so complicated? So, what to do? She decided, for the immediate danger, we go to Jeff's, with the understanding that it is a temporary situation. She went back into the house. Jeff and Haze were sound asleep on the couch. That's okay, I'm tired too. We can deal with this in the morning.

* * *

Clive was pissed, but there was nothing he could do about it, given his current situation. It wasn't as if he could have stopped the woman from taking her back. After all, he had taken her in the first place. He felt cheated, he was within reach of finding out the source of resurrection. If he had that knowledge, he could rule the world. His dreams had been dashed for now, but he would eventually find out. Once his leg is healed, all bets are off. First, he had to find out who those people were because her file says no relatives.

"Hopkins…. Hopkins!" He bellowed.

"I'm here! Stop yelling. It's annoying."

"Did you get the license plate off that truck?"

"Most of it. Should be easy enough to get an ID."

"Good. You can work on that, hopefully you can get a name!"

Chapter Seven
The Offer

Hope woke to the smell of bacon and fresh coffee brewing, no two better smells in the world. She couldn't wait to get up and investigate the source of those smells. She froze, *I'm excited to get up! When was the last time I've thought that?* Her life was changing yet again, and she was excited! Leaping out of bed, she got dressed, brushed her hair and snuck into the bathroom. When she was finished, she came out and stood in the doorway of the kitchen. Jeff was making eggs; no doubt to go with the bacon. She couldn't stop smiling.

Without looking up, he said, "I fed the animals after I gathered the eggs."

He said that it was a matter of fact like he said this every day. It took Hope by surprise. "Thank you, I'll bet they loved the early meal."

"Early! How late do you sleep?"

"Well… I normally sleep to seven, have my coffee and then feed the animals."

"I see" Jeff smiled. "And what time do you think it is now?"

"Early, isn't it?"

"Guess again. It's nearly ten o'clock!"

"No, really?"

"Have a look," he smiled. "It's your clock."

She looked at him, he was smiling like a Cheshire Cat who caught the mouse. She knew she was making the right decision.

Jeff removed the pan off the stove. "How a about you wake up sleeping beauty and you both come to the table!"

"You don't have to ask me twice. I'll be right back!"

Jeff was in his element, no doubt about it. This is his dream of how life should be, happy! He only hoped she would decide to go with him.

"Two hungry people coming through."

"Yes!" squealed Megan. "I'm very hungry!"

Jeff had the table set perfectly and now he was plating the food. "Perfect timing! Because I have food!"

The mood at the table was light and fun. Jeff teased Megan about eating with her fingers and in a few minutes, she actually started using a fork! He did it with such ease and that made the transition fun for her. She'll still need practice, but she will accomplish this too, just like everything else she tries.

When the kitchen was cleaned up. Megan asked, "Can I take Haze outside?"

"Sure! Do you want to feed her too?"

"Yes please."

Hope filled a baby bottle. Haze was eating like a mountain lion. It was impossible to fill her up these days as she was growing up so fast. She was at the toddler stage. Wanting to walk and run all at the same time, tripping and tumbling head over hills most of the time. She was definitely fun to watch. In another two weeks, she will go back to Mazey, where she will learn to hunt for herself. We will miss her terribly.

Jeff and Hope sat at the table with fresh cups of coffee. "I have made my decision and I think we must go with you for now, if the offer still stands."

"Yes, it does. Shall we talk it over with Megan? I don't want her to feel left out."

"Let's do it."

Once they were seated on the grass, Hope asked, "Megan, what do you think about us going to Jeff's Mountain home and staying there for a while."

She looked from Hope to Jeff. "Are we hiding again?"

Hope replied, "Yes…"

Megan stared at the ground for a few minutes before she said, "If we are going to be safe, yes."

"Well," said Hope. "Then we better get started."

The move wasn't difficult as Hope didn't have much to move. She explained to the Vicker that she would be away for a while and could he find someone to feed the animals. A perfect job for his son, he told her. She thanked him and in minutes they were headed to Jeff's. The further away they got away from the village, the better Hope felt. By the time they got to the farm, they were laughing, almost giddy.

As they climbed out of the truck, Jeff spread his arms and said, "Okay Ladies, home sweet home."

"Oh Jeff! This is stunning!"

"I built this house and barn myself."

"Impressive, Jeff. And look at the size of that garden, it's huge!"

"Yes, well I feed more than just me. There are people in Flatbush who don't have enough to eat. So, I take them fresh fruits and vegetables."

"Fruit!"

He pointed, "Over there behind the barn are six acres of fruit trees and wild berry bushes."

"Are you kidding me? This is amazing! I can make them preserves if you want. That will make the fruit go farther for the winter months. I just need small mason jars and paraffin wax."

"I'll get them when I go to work tomorrow."

"Do you have a big cooking pot?"

"You could come inside and see for yourself."

Megan yelped when she saw Cumba coming out of the barn, "Cumba! Can I go and see him?"

"Of course, you can," said Jeff. "I'm sure he would love to see you. We will be in the house. Don't leave the property, okay."

"I won't, I promise!"

When Hope walked inside the house, she was flabbergasted. Although the house did need a woman's touch, the house was enormous. It was neat and clean, not at all like the bachelor pads she heard about by some of women in town.

"Well, what do you think? Do you think you could live here?"

"Are you kidding me! The kitchen alone seals the deal! Look at the size of this kitchen! This would be so easy to work in and the amount of cooking I could do!"

"So glad you like it. I'm going to move into the spare room, you and Megan take the big bed."

Hope gratefully said, "Thank you."

It seemed like only minutes before he was bringing in their luggage. She went to the back door. "Megan, will you come here please."

"Sure." Immediately, Megan appeared in the kitchen.

"Jeff brought in our luggage, I would appreciate it if you would hang up our clothes so we can pick berries and apples when you're finished. How does that sound?"

"Okay, and after we do all the picking stuff, can I play with Cumba? He likes it when I play catch with him…"

"Catch? What are you using for a ball?"

"Apples…do you think Jeff could get him a ball?"

"You can ask him, if you'd like, but chores first, then play."

Megan ran for the bedroom, while Hope scoured the kitchen cupboards looking for pots, utensils, and sugar. Now to find baskets. She paused in mid-stride; and thought, *I feel like I belong here!*

* * *

Clive gritted his teeth as he took his first steps. The pain was horrific, and he had to sit down.

"It will get better," the therapist told him.

Liar, he thought, but nodded in agreement. When he was finished, Hopkins picked him up.

"I hope you have news for me…" said Clive rather sharply.

Sitting Clive down in his recliner, Hopkins smiled, "I do."

"Well, are you going to tell me, or do I have to guess?"

"Therapy didn't go well I take it."

"Shut up," he growled. "Tell me what you found out."

"The license plate belongs to Jeff Olsen. He's a zookeeper."

"The zoo in Flatbush?"

"Yes…"

"Interesting…can you toss the place when he's not home."

"Yeah, I think so."

"The sooner the better. If you don't find something that tells me where she is, bring him to me. Now let's eat, I'm starved."

* * *

Jeff literally sang every song that came on the radio all the way to Flatbush. The store was so delighted that there was preserves and soup. He promised he'd bring more when it was ready.

When he left the house, Hope was baking bread, pots of jam on the stove, and vegetable soup from the garden. The house smelled wonderful. He couldn't wait to get back to Hope and Megan. He did have to stop by his tiny apartment to get clothes and toiletries. He'd get the mason jars and paraffin on his lunch hour. That way he'd only need ten minutes to grab his things. *Great plan*, he thought and pulled into his parking slot at the zoo.

He was shocked how well his day went. There were no emergencies with the animals plus they were extra well behaved. *Interesting*, he thought, *that never happens. One of the large animals always acts up. Not that I blame them, Bradley is a bastard. He doesn't give a damn about them, only what they could do for him. One day, he'll get his comeuppance and I hope I'm there to see it.*

Lunchtime arrived and he drove to Hank's Feed & Grain. He bought every mason jar they had, which was eleven cases. They asked why he needed so many. He told the owners, Hank and Alice, that he and Hope were making food for the village of Flatbush. They promised to have more cases in by Friday and he'd could come by on his way home.

"Thank you," he said and then he hugged them both. They were an incredible couple. Hank was a large muscular man, no doubt from throwing hay bales and three-hundred-pound sacks of seed all day. Alice is a weaver and when she can get the heavy yarn, she makes beautiful blankets for the needy.

Back at work, he made sure every animal pen was spotless and all the animals had fresh food and water. The weather was heating up and the small animals like birds suffer terribly in the heat. *I really need to finish the sanctuary before the summer heat hits.*

Thank goodness his apartment was near the end of town, *a quick in and out and home, he thought.* Just the thought of home, which now included Hope and Megan, thrilled him.

He bounded up the stairs, key in hand and the door was cracked open. He stopped in front of the door and listened. No sounds could be heard inside. *Okay…I'll just get what I need and leave.* He opened the door slowly and stepped inside. There was nothing out of place! He looked toward the dinette and then the bed. Nothing was moved. He got what he needed and stepped outside. Making sure the door was locked before he went down the stairs to the truck. Before he turned the key, he glanced up at his apartment. Someone cased his apartment; they were looking around for what…information? His first thought was Clive Jenkins! Somehow, they found me, and they want me to know it. Nothing else makes sense. But I didn't go inside the institute, so how did they find me? Of course, my license plate!

He turned the key and hit the road. Hope is going to be very upset when she hears this. Her beautiful smile will fade into worry. In one day, that man has stripped us of our happiness. Jeff felt cheated and very angry.

He rounded the curve and thought he saw the front end of a truck behind him. He quickly drove deep into a thicket and turned off the engine. He got out of the truck and ducked down and listened. Sure enough, a truck drove by, and Hopkins was behind the wheel! He was the one I saw come outside the institute and I'll bet he memorized my plate number! I asked Hope, at the time, who he was, and she said his name tag said J. Hopkins.

Okay think, Jeff. It's an hour more to the farm and I doubt they will drive that whole way without seeing me. My guess is that they will turn around soon and come back. Patience, Jeff, just plain ole patience.

Thirty to forty minutes later the truck drove past, no doubt headed back toward town. Jeff got back into the truck and waited a few extra minutes, just to make sure he was gone. He backed out of the thicket and hit the gas. The minute he drove down the driveway, he headed for the barn and closed one of the barn doors. No one could see the truck hidden in the barn from the street. He took a deep breath to calm down and started unloading the supplies. Hope and Megan came out to help.

She noticed the damage to the truck but said nothing. Maybe, he'll tell me later, right now there's chores to do. The soup was cool enough to fill the jars and I have enough for supper.

"This meal is amazing, Hope."

"I used those vegetables that look like skinny cucumbers."

"That's okra and a good choice for soups!"

"I have no idea what okra is, but it does add a little different flavor and I like it."

"Okra is a vegetable grown mainly in the southeastern part of the states. I hear tell down there they eat it like candy!"

"Now you're joking with me…"

"Maybe just a little, but he did say that they put it in every dish."

She chuckled, "Now that I believe. Want to help me jar up the apple sauce?"

"Love too. What about the preserves?"

"I need more to cook. I don't think I have enough for everyone. Wait how many people are in Flatbush?"

"Well now, I think about twenty, amongst six families."

"Twenty huh, if I make half jars that should do. Tomorrow, Megan and I will get more, but I'll have to out along the road for a little way."

"No, you can't!"

Hope was startled by the sharp tone of his voice and instantly angered. "Excuse me, who do you think you're talking to in that tone of voice? Not me!"

"I'm sorry…sit down please." She did. "I had a couple of surprises today and they weren't pleasant."

"Okay…continue."

"My apartment was gone through, and I was followed, but I lost them a long way back."

"Clive?"

"No Hopkins…"

"So, they're already at it."

"It seems so."

Megan busted through the door. "It's because of me! And they're gonna try to take me away again, aren't they? Well, I'm not going anywhere! Nowhere!" She burst into tears and ran to the bedroom.

They just looked at each other and headed to the bedroom.

Hope picked her up and hugged her real tight. "We didn't mean to upset you. I forgot you can hear us from outside."

"I don't hear live people's words only dead people and animals. I feel emotions, like if you're scared. And you were scared."

Jeff said, "Yes, I was and I'm sorry you felt that. But, to answer you, yes, they are looking for you, but we knew they would keep trying. That's why I came up with a plan. Do you want to hear it?"

The sniffling Megan looked up. "Okay…"

"I can make you a special room like you had before."

"You can?"

"Yes, I can. There is a basement here and I can build it really easy."

She stopped crying. "I can tell you how."

"Perfect! So do you like my plan?"

"Yes!"

"Okay let's get busy."

Megan tried to smile, "Okay."

Jeff and Megan spent the rest of the evening and most of the next day finishing the room. Hope made blueberry tarts as a treat for them finishing the project. When they came upstairs. Hope covered the opening to the basement with a thick braided rug and Jeff replaced the table and chairs.

Hope stood back and looked at the arrangement. "It's going to take too much time to get her down there and replace the table."

"Yes, it will. We could rearrange the kitchen so that we are just lifting the rug and door."

Once the kitchen was swapped around, Hope felt that this configuration would work. "Perfect!"

Jeff was heading for the tarts cooling on the racks. "Now can I have a tart? I've been smelling them all day."

Megan practiced getting in and out of the basement until she could do it easily. That put her mind at ease.

"Can I go to the barn? Cumba and I are going to take a nap. We're tired…"

"Of course. We'll come and get you for dinner."

Megan left the house, and they watched her until she disappeared.

Hope squinted at Jeff, "Okay tell me about yesterday and I want every detail."

"First, I need to apologize for my tone, I was frightened for what could happen if they found you both."

"Thank you, but please don't ever talk to me like that again."

"I won't, I promise…"

"Okay apology accepted. Now spill…"

Jeff told her every detail that he could remember. "All the way home, I couldn't help but think that these people are crazy and dangerous, that's what has me frightened. Because I think I know what he wants."

Hope leaned in. "You do?"

"Yes," whispered Jeff. "He sees dollar signs when he looks at her. People would pay a fortune to be healed completely."

"Oh wow!" Hope's eyes widened. "You're right…they would! And he would exploit her, much like Cumba was exploited. He can't learn to do what she does. It's not something that can be learned. It's a gift only she has."

Jeff was puzzled, "I don't understand, gift?"

"I think the reason Megan is able to heal is because she has a pure heart or has pure intention, something like that…she is an open vessel filled with love. Haven't you noticed that nothing really fazes her for more than a minute. When something bad happens she calmly handles whatever needs to be done, and when the crisis is over, she acts like it never happened."

"Well… no…I hadn't noticed, but I will in the future. We cannot let him get a hold of her… ever!"

"Not ever." Hope repeated. "We have an hour or so before dinner, shall we finish canning?"

"Yes, I'll drop them off in the morning. They will be so thrilled!" He hesitated, "I think I should stay in town for a while."

Her heart broke, "Why? Did I do something wrong?"

"No! I'm afraid of leading them here, that's all. You are perfect." He instantly blushed.

She grabbed him and held him close. She whispered in his ear, "You are perfect too."

Chapter Eight
Hopkins

There is no way Hopkins wanted to walk in Clive's office without Jeff Olsen in tow, but he had no choice. He'd driven up and down that road a dozen times and couldn't find out where he went. There wasn't an old truck in any of the driveways; most of the trucks were newer.

In lieu of facing Clive, he went to dinner at El Guano's Bar and Grill. They have the best guacamole, salsa, and enchiladas anywhere in two counties. While he ate, he tried to figure out how Jeff disappeared. There weren't that many places to hide along that road. He must live in one of those houses, but I checked every driveway and there aren't any houses farther out, only old mining shacks. *Tomorrow I'll try again*, he thought. *Right now, I have to face Clive and it ain't going to be pretty.*

He paid the bill and headed to the office. Clive was eating when he walked in.

"I see you're empty handed."

"Yes, I am. I lost him on Baluster Road."

"There isn't anything out there but orchards and mining shacks."

"Yes, I know…I'll try again tomorrow."

"Okay…."

"See you later." Hopkins couldn't wait to get away from him. He is a miserable man.

Unfortunately, sleep escaped Hopkins. He paced most of the night and when he finally laid down and closed his eyes, he had nightmares. At five in the morning, he gave up on sleep and decided to stake out the road where it enters town. He settled in the grocery store parking lot, which was vacant at this hour of the morning. He had a thermos of coffee and a ham and egg sandwich. *I'll be good for a while. He'd better show up.*

At eight o'clock, he hadn't seen Jeff and decided to move over to his job sight. Another hour goes by, and Jeff finally shows up. He relaxed just knowing where he was. *I'll be back at quitting time*, for now he needed to sleep. When he got home, he set the alarm for three in the afternoon.

At four o'clock, he was parked inconspicuously at the zoo. He had to find a way to grab him without being seen. The parking lot was nearly empty, so why not here? I can just pull up, put a gun in his side, and zip, he's off to visit Clive. Here he comes!

Jeff climbed into his truck and the next thing he knew; Hopkins was standing at his window holding a gun.

"Get out we're going for a ride," ordered Hopkins.

"Really?"

"Yes really!" The instant Hopkins opened Jeff's door; Jeff shoved the door hard into Hopkins' chest which knocked him off his feet. Jeff started the truck and took off with tires squealing.

It took a minute for Hopkins to regain his breath. He got up off the ground pissed, embarrassed, and determined to get the bastard.

Jeff drove as fast as he dared. Turning onto the road that would take him home, he prayed he was far enough ahead of Hopkins so that he couldn't follow him.

Pulling into the garage and closing the door, he ran for the house. Hope was baking and Megan was nowhere in sight.

"Megan, where is she?"

"Napping! What's wrong?"

"Hopkins is what's wrong! He tried to kidnap me today! He held me at gun point!"

"And you got away…do I want to know what you did?"

"He's still alive if that's what you're asking…"

"No, I meant what did you have to do to get away?"

"Oh, that was easy. When he went to open my door, I shoved the door as hard as I could, and he landed on the ground with the wind knocked out of him! I hightailed it home to check on you to make sure you both were alright."

Hope sat down at the table. "Is this ever going to end?"

"Yes, it will. I'm going to make sure it does…"

"How?"

"Let him catch me…."

"No! I will not lose you, too!"

"You will not lose me, I promise."

"How can you promise that?"

"Easy, I was in Special Forces. Those two idiots can't hurt me."

"I don't know what Special Forces means…"

Oh crap! She's never watched TV shows or the news, so she wouldn't know what I'm talking about. "Okay, let me try to explain it. I was in the military for fifteen years and I was trained to survive in jungles for prolonged periods of time and in the deserts too. I have Special skills in various forms of martial arts. I am extremely trained to be deadly in combat. Those two bozos do not stand a chance against me. Does that help?"

"I have heard about the military, some of the men in the villages have served. I just never listened to their war stores. The women say they are gruesome."

"Yes, they can be…those guys served in the regular army. I was trained to extract captured prisoners, the bigger stuff."

"So, you're saying that you can handle yourself against Clive and Hopkins both at the same time?"

"Yes, I am. I swear no harm will come to me. Well maybe a bloody nose or a scratch or two."

"Okay…I believe you," she conceded. "Now get back to town…remember, you're not supposed to be here today. I have laundry to do, and I don't want you seeing my undergarments flapping in the breeze…"

He almost laughed aloud. "As you wish Milady!"

She hugged him tightly. "I don't wish, but I do understand."

Jeff ran to his truck and headed back to town. His apartment had everything he needed to protect himself. Watching the parking lots and side streets that led up to his apartment complex, he was sure Hopkins' truck wasn't around, but it will be, no doubt about that.

On the bottom floor, was an exceptionally good Chinese restaurant, where he ate often. But before he went down, he armed himself with a shive knife strapped to his leg. In his coat pocket, he put a small 22 pistol. Satisfied that he had protection, he went downstairs and took the table against the wall closest to the window. When Mi'ling came to take his order, he placed it in her native tongue, Cantonese. She bowed deeply and left his table.

The wonderful thing about Chinese food is that it's ready in minutes. Any other day he'd care about how long it took until his food arrived, he was usually starving, but not today. He decided on the drive here that the only way they could be safe is to kill them both.

There were two exits in here, only one in his apartment; not a good advantage to go upstairs. His food arrived and he began to eat, never taking his eyes off the window. He was nearly finished when Hopkins truck entered the parking lot. He drove very slowly past Jeff's truck and pulled into a slot at the end of the row. Jeff wished he could be a fly on the wall to find out what he's up to. No doubt he's talking to himself out loud right about now. I know I would be. Let's just see what he does first because that will dictate what's going to happen next.

Jeff didn't have to wait long. Hopkins got out of his truck and walked down the sidewalk passed Jeff's truck. When he got to the end of the block, he turned around and walked back. He's casing the place.

Jeff became suddenly aware that Hopkins could be black op or probably a mercenary operative. Once that thought entered the picture, Jeffs game plan changed. He will have to draw him away from here. Too many people could get hurt or worse get caught in the crossfire. Thank goodness, he had heavy fire power in his truck.

Hopkins was rummaging around his truck looking for something, and Hopkin's back was toward him. He threw money on the table and bolted to his truck, started the engine, and took off. Hopkins didn't notice until he looked up and he saw Jeff's taillights leaving the parking lot. Not what he wanted to see.

Jeff kept looking in his review mirror until he saw Hopkins come out of the parking lot. Jeff sped up. Hopkins matched his speed easily. *"Okay,* thought Jeff, *the chase is on*! Once they left the city limits, Jeff headed toward Flatbush, and doubled his speed.

Halfway to town, Hopkins tried to hit the left corner of Jeff's bumper. The result would be Jeff spinning around and possibly rolling over. Jeff sped up so Hopkins missed his mark. Hopkins was coming at him again and when he was about to hit the bumper, Jeff slammed on his brakes. Hopkins hit the back of Jeff's truck so hard that the hitch went through Hopkins' radiator. *Perfec*t, Jeff though!

Because of the high speeds they've been traveling, when the radiator punctured, Hopkins truck looked like a steamy fountain of youth. He had to stop or blow his motor. Now Hopkins was stranded out in the middle of nowhere! Jeff smiled and kept driving.

He drove through Flatbush and headed toward Flatbottom Lake where he could hide the truck behind wild blackberry bushes, his favorite napping spot. I'll see what Hopkins has in store for me tomorrow. No doubt he'll come at me with a vengeance.

Sometime after midnight, Jeff was awakened by someone calling his name. "Who's there?" No response. He sat up and looked in all directions, no one. Then he felt it…**tug**! Megan's dad! What was his name, Gary, no that's not it. He thought for a minute, Garrett!

"Garrett, is this you?" **Tug!** "Okay, is there a problem with Megan or Hope?" **Tug, tug.**

His blanket was being pulled off.

"Do you want me to get out of the truck?" **Tug!**

He didn't have to be told twice. He gathered his blanket, pillow, and gun. Garrett had ahold of his shirt and led him away, but not far enough that he couldn't see his truck. It didn't take but a minute before Jeff saw a figure crouched down skirting the picnic area. He was heading toward the truck! How could he possibly find me? There was only one way and he had to put a tracker on the truck at the restaurant! So that's why he got out and walked around the parking lot! You're slipping old man or you're underestimating your opponent. Jeff felt a nudge at his side and looked down at Loki! Patting the wolf on the head, Jeff kept an eye on Hopkins' movements. He was near the truck now and Jeff wanted to see his face when he discovered that there was no one inside.

"Son of a bitch!" He yelled. "He has to be around here somewhere." With that, Hopkins entered the woods. Mazey and a large male wolf, that Jeff hadn't noticed, went to the right paralleling Hopkins. *Oh man, that poor bastard!* He thought. With Garrett and the wolves following him, he will be dead meat in a matter of minutes.

Then Jeff heard, "What's the problem Garrett? Did you lose her again?"

"No…"

"Then where is she? Back up will you, you're too cold. Come on dude, back up! I'm freezing…"

Hopkins started to swing his arms around as if to get Garrett off of him, without success. That's when Jeff saw the wolves crouch to spring!

Oh no, I don't want to hear this. He ran to his truck, turned the key, and that's when he heard Hopkins' first scream. Jeff hit the gas pedal and got out of there as fast as he could. It will be a while before they find his body. And, by the time they do, he will have fed the whole forest. Jeff shuddered. One down one to go!

Chapter Nine
Clive's Revenge

When Clive left the rehab center, he expected to see Hopkins waiting for him, he wasn't there. He waited for an hour! Where is he? Damn, now I'm going to have to call for a taxi. Hopkins is going to rue the day he abandoned me. *Stupid bastard*, he thought. *He's on his last legs with me anyway. I'm done coddling his ass.*

"Hey driver could you go through the drive through at Harley's Burgers for me?"

"Sure fella, what do you want?"

He gave the driver his order and a handful of bills. When they arrived at the office, the driver helped him inside and set him up at the kitchen table.

"Thanks..." and handed him a twenty-dollar tip.

"You're welcome, sir. Will you'll be alright now?"

"Yes, I will be fine."

Hopkins wouldn't just abandon me. He would call me if something happened. Chive decided to call his home again and still had no answer. Surely, he'd go to that restaurant he loves so much and dialed that number. After a dozen calls and several inquiries, no one had seen or heard from him this week.

Three days later, without any communication from Hopkins and a million unanswered messages, he was worried enough that he called the sheriff's department to report him missing. They would send someone out tomorrow to take his report.

Clive rolled around the office so much that there were rubber marks on the floor. He couldn't take being shut in one more minute, so he called a taxi. While he waited, he decided that he could do some surveillance on his own. *No,* he thought, *that's stupid. But on the other hand, why not? I'm just looking for Jeff's truck, right? I can do that much from a taxi!*

The driver pulled up and he leaped out to assist Clive into the cab.

Looking at his name tag, which read Ben Walters, Clive asked, "Are you in a hurry Ben, because I want to drive around for a bit this evening?"

"No rush here, sir."

"Perfect…"

Once Clive was comfortable in the taxi, the driver asked, "Where to first?"

"Have you had dinner?"

"No sir."

"Do you like Chinese food?"

"Yes, I do."

"There's a really good restaurant on Fountain Street have you eaten there?"

"Chang's, yes sir, a time or two. It's very good."

"Let's start there."

"Yes sir."

Just as Clive hoped, Jeff's truck was in the lot. The lights were on in Jeff's apartment. Because of the late hour, it was unlikely that Jeff would be eating there. The restaurant was crowded, which made Clive very happy. At a glance, Jeff wouldn't be able to pick him out so readily in a crowd.

Dinner was superb as always. Clive paid the bill and Ben loaded him up in the taxi. Ben jumped in the driver's seat as Jeff was coming down the stairs.

"Hold on a minute. I want to see where this guy is headed."

"You know him?"

"Yes, he owes me for a side job I did a while back."

"How fortuitous, running into him. Do you want me to stop him?"

"No, I have people to do the collecting. Let's just see where he goes, and I'll pass the information to them. I'm in no condition to confront him as it could become volatile."

"I see, I was a repo man in Pittsburgh many years ago. So, I get it."

"So, you *do* understand."

"Yes sir."

The problem with small towns is that it's hard to tail people. You really need traffic to remain inconspicuous. Clive wanted to follow Jeff without being seen, but it was nearly impossible. Tonight, traffic was nonexistent. *Well, we can try for a bit and then turn left at the time when Jeff might be getting suspicious.*

"Let's follow him for a little bit, if he slows, turn off onto a side street."

"Sure thing."

Jeff's truck left the parking lot and turned right. Interesting, thought Clive. The only thing in that direction is Flatbush!

"Ben wait a minute. This taxi is too conspicuous, how about we take my truck? You drive, of course. I'll pay you for your time instead. How about a hundred bucks an hour? Does that sound fair?"

"Yes, sir very fair."

They switched vehicles and headed for Flatbush. "Let's go, and Ben …and my name is Charles, but I prefer Charlie."

"Charlie it is. Hey, are you affiliated with that institute?"

"No…the real estate office next door. I know, boring as hell, but it pays the bills!"

"I've always been curious; do you know what they do in there?"

"I've heard from some of the other tenants in the complex, that it has something to do with the study of telepathy and paranormal. I don't understand that kind of thinking, myself."

"Me either. Hey, we're coming up nearing Flatbush! Okay, slow down and cruise the street looking for his truck."

"No problem, he's right in front of the feed and grain store."

"Okay, let's park at the ribs place and in the back row."

"Sure, you don't want him to see you…"

"No, that's not it. He wouldn't recognize me as we've never met."

"I thought…"

"Yes, when we did the side job, the only person he met with was my associate and now he is missing."

"I see, so why the cloak and dagger stuff?"

"You know, I really don't know. I think I feel better with him not knowing who I am. I'm a bit of an introvert and I'm not comfortable around people that was Jerry's job. I'm good on the phone. Sounds crazy, right?"

"No…, so why real estate?"

"That's easy, estate sales. Those bring in good money and I can send my associate to meet with the clients."

"That makes perfect sense!"

"With Jerry missing, I don't know what to do, I'm stuck."

"Any ideas on what you can do?"

"Naw, but something will show up and I can do more side jobs that I will occupy my time."

"Yes, you mentioned them before. He's getting in his truck. What do you want to do?"

"Follow him for a bit, I want to see where he goes next."

When they neared town, Clive sat forward, "Okay let's keep our eyes on his truck."

"He seems to be going back to his apartment."

"Okay, we'll I'm getting tired take me back to my place. Hey Ben, will you pick me up tomorrow at the rehab center?"

"Sure thing."

"Great thanks, here's the address." Clive wrote it down on a receipt he had in his pocket and handed it to Ben. Clive paid Ben what he promised and went inside. He was furious that he couldn't capture Jeff. But in two weeks he'll be fair game.

Two weeks passed rather quickly, and Clive felt fit as a fiddle. Now he just needed Jeff to slip up and lead him to Megan. He felt he'd been patient long enough.

Chapter Ten
Discovery

Jeff delivered Hope's preserves and soup to the feed store and picked up more jars and wax. With Hopkins out of the way he was more relaxed, although Clive was still out there, he felt safer somehow. The one thing he wasn't sure of was, will Clive take up where Hopkins left off. It's been a month and no inklings that he was being watched or stocked.

With the deliveries made, he was ready to head home. The ease in which the blending of our two lifestyles worked perfectly. No bickering or squabbles ever interfered with their goals, keeping Megan safe and feeding Flatbush. Hope worked so hard as not to waste one berry or a single carrot. She was as close to perfect as one woman could get and he had to admit, he loved her with his whole heart.

But in the back of his mind the thought of Clive kept creeping in. He's still out there plotting who knows what. What is he up to? He's been quiet far too long which put Jeff on alert more and more each day. It was as if he was becoming paranoid and he hated that feeling. A trap was about to be sprung and he needed to be ready. But right this minute, he wanted to revel in how perfect his life is and hoped it would stay that way. He patted his shirt pocket where the ring box sat safely tucked inside. Hopefully, she'll say yes!

Pulling into the barn, he saw Hope and Megan working in the garden. His heart filled with joy just watching them. He hopped out of the truck and walked over to see if he could help.

"Hi ladies need some muscle to carry anything?"

"Hi, I didn't hear you pull in!"

"Hi Jeff!" Megan got up to hug him. "You're just in time to carry these baskets please."

"Gladly, my you have been busy!"

"The vegetables are ripping all at once. I've got to pick them before they spoil."

"I'll get more baskets after I take this inside. Let me wash the zoo off of me and I'll help with the harvest. How does that sound?"

"Perfect! Thank you. I'll make us some lemonade." Hope headed for the house and thought that her life was perfect.

Hope turned on the radio to listen to her favorite music station. Jeff had shown her that music made the soul happy, and she had to agree.

"Breaking news," the announcer said. "A body was found near Flatbottom Lake by a hiker. The identification is unknown at this time. Speculation is that this could be a man that was reported missed several months ago."

Hope froze and turned around; Jeff was standing in the doorway. All the color was drained from his face, and he was sweating.

Hope had to ask, "Could this be Hopkins?"

Jeff nodded. He told her what happened between them and made it clear to her that he did not kill him. "Only one problem, if this body turns out to be Hopkins, Clive will point a finger at me. So be prepared to be interviewed by the police."

"Will we be, okay?" Whispered Hope.

"Should be. There isn't a human hand that can be associated with his death."

"Okay then, let's continue with the harvest."

Jeff only nodded and lifted the tray of lemonade. Outside, he felt he could breathe. He was sure the body they found would turn out to be Hopkins. His proposal will have to wait.

The harvest was complete for today. The kitchen was lined with eighteen-bushel baskets full of fresh vegetables and only a couple of them were berries. The full crop of berries and fruit won't be ready until next month. Hope will have all of this cooked up and jarred in no time.

Megan and Jeff came in from the barn, no doubt making sure the animals were all tucked in for the night. It was their nightly ritual.

"Dinner will be ready in an hour," informed Hope. "Plenty of time for you to get cleaned up."

"Yes ma'am:" Megan wanted to know, "Can I go first?"

"Sure…and when you get out of the bathroom, will you set the table please?"

"Yes, I can do that." She ran to the bedroom.

Hope pounded the beef steak until it was tender.

Jeff came into the kitchen all cleaned up. "Can I help with dinner?"

"Sure, you can peel potatoes…" *she said nearly in a whisper.*

That's when he noticed her hands were trembling, he immediately took her in his arms. She crumbled against him.

He whispered in her ear, "We will be fine, I promise."

"You can't promise that with Clive out there! You just said, Clive will blame you!"

"Let him try. I did not kill Hopkins!"

"I know, but…"

"No buts," he interrupted her. "Megan is coming out of the bathroom. Can we talk later? Besides, if we are going to eat tonight, I need to peel potatoes."

"Yes later…."

When dinner was over and the kitchen cleaned, Megan asked, as she did every night, if she could go to the barn to play with Cumba.

Jeff and Hope sat down and held hands across the table. "Jeff, I'm afraid…"

"I know, but aren't we jumping the gun a bit? We have no idea what's going to happen. Until they're through with the investigation and announce their findings, we are in the clear. There is a long way to go yet, so don't worry."

"Could we be so lucky as to not get caught up in Hopkins death?"

"How could we be involved? There is no link between him and me. Plus, he shouldn't have any human link to his death at all."

She had to think about that for a moment, "Okay, I will put aside my fears for now."

"Great!" Jeff paused for a minute. "Now there is another matter to talk about…"

"There is?"

"Yes," reaching in his pocket, he pulled out the ring box. "Hope, will you marry me?"

Hope was astonished! She instantly started crying… "Yes, I would be honored."

Jeff leapt up to pull her out of the chair, he felt desperate to hold her. They were crying. Megan came flying into the kitchen and saw them crying.

"What's happened? What's wrong?" She was frantic, looking from one to the other.

He knelt down in front of her, so their eyes met, "Nothing is wrong! Everything is right! What would you say if Hope and I got married? That way we could be a real family!"

"Me too?"

"Yes, you, too. See after we're married, we can adopt you as our very own! What do you think about that?"

"No one can take me away?"

"No one, you would belong to us and we would become your parents!"

Megan stood there, barely breathing, so afraid that even though all of this could be true, Clive could take her away. He did it before. She frowned, and blurted, "Clive could take me away again."

"Megan…no….no…. I'll protect you from him. But what we meant is that by adopting you, no one can take you away from us."

She seemed to snap back, "Yes, yes, I'll be so happy to be your daughter."

"Good, you had us worried."

"I need to talk to my dad first."

"Of course!"

* * *

Knowing definitely that the body they found at Flatbottom Lake was indeed Hopkins, put Clive on notice that Jeff was someone dangerous. However, it would be a few days before the coroner would have the autopsy completed.

The only thing he knew for sure was right about the time of his disappearance, he was following Jeff day and night. Maybe they had a confrontation, or he got too close to Megan. The scenarios were endless. He had to know what happened. He picked up the phone to call the coroner and then decided not to, it wouldn't help him get the results any faster.

The next day, the morning newscaster said the autopsy results for the body of Jerald Hopkins will be ready and revealed on the twelve o'clock broadcast. Clive paced nonstop, unable to sit down and wait the last hour until the news came on. So many thoughts ran through his mind as he contemplated what the decision of murder would mean. Of course, they would interview him, he was his employer. What will I say? That I sent him to follow Jeff and maybe something happened between them, and they ask why I sent him? That won't work. I better figure out a story to tell them and soon.

Finally, the twelve o'clock news was about to begin, and he turned on the TV.

The newscaster began by saying; "Do to the graphic nature of this report, viewer discretion is advised." Okay, he thought and took a deep breath before he continued. "Ben Calderon, County Corner for Haynes County. Doctor Caldron...."

"I performed the autopsy on Jerald Hopkins and what I found was disturbing. Mr. Hopkins was mauled by wolves and suffered a horrendous death."

"Wolves! Are you sure?"

"Yes, positive. I matched the teeth marks on the bones."

"Couldn't the marks have been done after his death?"

"No." the doctor swallowed something invisible. "He was ripped apart while he was still alive, and I know that by the blood staining on the bones. I was sure it would be homicide myself! But not this time. This is murder by wolf!"

"Thank you. Next up the hunt for the murderous wolves."

Clive didn't know what to think, so he sat down in his chair. *Murder by wolf!*

Chapter Eleven
Wolf Hunt

Hope wasn't shocked by the autopsy report. She was sure Mazey's pack kill Hopkins and now they will be hunted. She had to find out what the authorities were going to do to capture them and figure out what they could do to save them.

Jeff and Megan came busting through the back door. Megan was frantic, "Mazey is in trouble! We have to save her…"

"I know…can you talk to her or are you feeling her emotions?"

"Both… Should they come toward us?"

"No, that's too direct. They will be seen." Jeff grabbed the truck keys. "It would be easier for them to go to Flatbush, but not inside the town. Tell them there are woods they can hide in and be safe. I'm on my way. Tell them to go now!"

"Okay I did."

Jeff hugged her. "Thanks…!"

The newscaster and the sheriff were about to discuss what plans they were making to kill all the wolves in the area.

In an interview, the sheriff was grim as he said, "I'm going on record to say that never have wolves attacked a human in this manner. With that said, we have organized search parties to track and kill all the wolves. We do not want citizens going out and trying to find them. Please let us do the tracking. We have several expert trackers already on site working the scene."

The reporter asked, "Are you focusing on a particular area?"

"Yes, Flatbottom Lake where the murder occurred and span out from there. We are confident we will find them quickly."

The reporter grimaced, "You are so sure…"

"Yes, this is not a roving ban of wolves. These, I believe, are local."

Hope turned off the broadcast and looked at Megan. "You, okay?"

"Yes, Mazey says they've left the den."

"Good. We need to figure out where would be the best place to hide them."

"Jeff's zoo would be the best place, but Mazey says no way."

Hope chuckled, "I'm not surprised she objected. Although the zoo would be a great idea if the boss wasn't there."

Megan's eyes lit up and Hope caught the look and instantly said, "Oh no you don't young lady! Only for good remember?"

Megan frowned, "I wasn't going to hurt him. just make him very sick, so he has to leave for a while."

"There are other workers." Hope told her then asked, "Are going to make all of them all sick?"

"I could…"

Hope crossed her arms, "I'm sure you could but let's not, okay?"

"Okay…"

"Let me know the instant Jeff has them, please and maybe we should find a place to put them. Where do we start?"

"Cumba will know where to make a den."

"Perfect! Let's go and ask him!"

As the three companions scouted the woods behind the orchards, Cumba would randomly stop and sniff the air. Megan noticed his odd behavior and asked him why he kept smelling the air? Fire, he told her. Is it close? No, was his reply.

Cumba stopped and pawed the underbrush by a six-foot high pile of large rocks.

"Cumba this is perfect! We just need to make it bigger."

Megan shook her head, "He says deeper."

"Well then, we need the backhoe. Wait here while I go and get it."

It took a while for Hope to return with the backhoe because she got lost. She had never ventured out passed the orchards. Here in the woods, she was not familiar with the small knolls that seemed to be everywhere, and they all looked alike. *I really have to pay better attention and not get distracted by berry bushes and wild onions. I can harvest all these onions! What a find!*

Eventually she heard Megan hollering at her from the top of one of the knolls. "Thank goodness!"

Megan was laughing when she showed up. "You were lost!"

"Yes, I was…so, go ahead and laugh!"

"No, I laughed already." But she kept chuckling for a while.

Hope positioned the backhoe and set the jake-brake. Within thirty minutes, she had a deep cavern dug.

"What do you think Cumba, big enough for the whole pride?"

Cumba walked inside and was gone for a short time. When he came out, he walked away.

Hope looked at Megan, "What does that mean?"

"Big enough, but it needs hay."

"I brought some, it's on the back. That is the one thing I remembered from the den by Flatbottom."

"I'll spread it out on the inside, you're too big!"

"Thank you…"

They were on their way back to the barn when Megan hollered, "Stop!"

Hope stopped. "What is it, Megan?"

"I don't know for sure, cuz I'm getting pictures from Mazey. There's a man talking to Jeff and…" Megan's eyes widened, "Oh no! It's Clive!"

"Clive!" Hope eyes teared up instantly. "Anything else?"

"They're just talking. I told Mazey to stay out of sight and to be quite. She said she would."

Hope was beside herself with worry. "I'm going to go to the barn, it's getting dark."

"Okay, I'll tell you more when I see something."

"Okay…"

Hope put the backhoe back in the side of the barn that holds the farm equipment and closed the doors. She fell to the ground and sobbed. Megan came flying out of the house and found Hope in a heap on the ground. "Hope…Hope…it's okay." She sat down on the ground beside her and got as close as she could.

Hope hugged the small child. There was comfort holding Megan, real comfort. Hope had no idea how long they sat on the ground. It didn't matter.

"I think," Megan whispered, "that Mazey is in the truck."

"Think?"

"Yes, I think so."

"That means Jeff got away from Clive!"

"I think so…, yes he did!" Megan jumped up. "Jeff is really hungry and so is Mazey!"

Hope sat up. "Jeff is easy, but the wolves won't be!"

"What do we do?"

"I don't know…" Hope stood up and looked at her dress. "I've got to get cleaned up, I'm a mess!"

Megan's dress was soiled from crawling around the new den. "Me too!"

Both women ran for the house. Hope let Megan go first while she started dinner. *What in the world can I feed the wolves?*

***

Jeff finished shopping at the feed store and had piled everything at the back door. He was walking out to pull his truck around to the back for loading. Clive walked in!

"Jeff, how are you?"

Jeff just stood there blinking.

"I don't think we've actually met, I'm Clive Jenkins."

He fanned non-recognition of his name. "I'm sorry, I don't recognize the name." He turned and tried to walk around him, but Clive sidestepped to block his path. "I suggest you move on your own or…"

"Or what? You're going to move me?"

Alice called from the register area, "Hey Jeff…Mac just called, his truck is broken down and asked if you would take this pile of supplies to him."

"Sure…I'll drive around to the dock." He never took his eyes off Clive while he talked with Alice. He stood inches from Clive's face as he said in an even tone, "Move…"

Clive just smiled…Jeff brought up his elbow in a ratcheting motion and dropped Clive where he stood. He stepped over him and went to his truck, drove around back, thanked Alice, and loaded his truck.

"Give me a few minutes head start before you try to revive him."

"Gladly, now you get and hug Hope for us."

"Will do!" Jeff drove to the edge of the woods and saw Mazey running towards him. He opened the back, Mazey jumped in as Loki, Haze and a teenage wolf emerged out of the brush. "Mazey is this all that are going?"

Growl…growl…

"Okay girl…" he drove away and headed for home.

The drive home was nerve wracking. The constant looking over his shoulder or in the rearview mirrors for an unfamiliar vehicle. He had no idea what kind of car or truck he owned. He was relieved when the barn door closed behind him. Hope flew out the back door and into Jeff's arms.

"I thought he was going to force you into an altercation."

"He tried, but I knocked him out before he could. He'll be hunting for me now."

"What are we going to do? You have to go to work!"

"I know…not sure yet. I need to think about it first. Okay Mazey wants out!"

"I almost forgot about her!"

Jeff went to the rear of the truck and opened the hatch and lowered the tailgate. Mazey and the others jumped out.

Megan yelled, "Mazey!" As she came running out the back door.

The wolf looked toward the house and ran to Megan. After what seemed like an eternity, they both walked over to Jeff and Hope.

"Mazey says they barely got away from the men with guns."

Hope turned to Mazey. "We are going to feed you and take you to your new home, okay?"

"She says hurry up with the food!"

Hope ran for the house and returned with a trough like bowl. Megan, there are more of these in the house.

Jeff asked, "What is this young wolf's name?"

"Tega, he is Mazey's son," Megan called out over her shoulder.

The wolves ate vigorously, it was obvious they hadn't eaten in a while and when they were finished, they laid down.

Megan sat down in front of them and said, "Tega, we welcome you to our home. We are sorry that you lost your den, but we have made you a new one, we hope you like it! When you're ready, we will take you to it. But before we take you, whatever you do, do not go beyond this area."

Jeff motioned for them to follow. Hope and Megan led them to the den.

Jeff whispered, "I can't wait to see what you two created!"

Hope whispered, "I just hope they like it."

Jeff hugged Hope, "We're about to find out."

Megan told Mazey that their den was right in front of them. Mazey looked at her like she was crazy. She began to investigate and found it immediately.

Human scent, Mazey said. That's what gave it away. She went inside and was gone for quite a while. When she finally came out, she licked Megan's face.

"She likes it!" All the wolves went inside, including Mazey.

On the walk back to the house, Megan asked, "Clive wants to hurt you. What can we do to stop him?"

"Right now, I don't know. I have two days to figure it out…I don't want you to worry."

"I am already worried. He is a very bad man!"

"Yes, he is, but guess what I am a very capable of avoiding his attempts to harm me!"

Megan was not interested in the grownup's conversation. "Can I play with Cumba?"

"Not yet, dinner will be ready in a matter of minutes. But after dinner you can."

"Okay I'll set the table."

"Excellent!" Hope gave her a squeeze. Megan went into the house. Hope stopped Jeff. "I have a ton of questions!"

"I know, but can I eat first?"

"Sure…"

The instant Megan finished her meal and cleaned her plate, she ran for the barn.

Jeff had been quiet throughout the meal. Hope put her hand on his arm, "Any ideas?"

"Lots but nothing that keeps him from hunting me. I'm sure he's really pissed right now."

"What happened?"

"He tried to stop me from leaving and I put him on the floor. He was still unconscious when I left."

"Yikes, did you break his nose?"

"Nope, his jaw."

For a split second, Hope wanted to cheer, but fear set in instead. "He's going to hunt you down to get even."

"Yes, he will. I've got a few ideas about work too. I can park inside. There are three exits, he can't be at all of them."

"Okay, promise me you'll keep an eye out and be ready for him."

"I promise. Now come here." Jeff held out his arms and she grabbed hold of him.

He held her trembling body tight against his until her tremors stopped. When they parted Megan was coming out of the barn.

Jeff seeing the sad look on Megan's face, asked, "Everything okay?"

"I don't know, I think Cumba hurts in his bones."

"Why do you say that?"

"Because he groans when he stands up."

"When I go to work, I'll look at his record to see how old he is. If he's over twenty, it could be arthritis."

"Is that bad?"

"It can be and it's very painful."

"Can we get medicine to help him?"

Jeff was confused! Why was she asking for medicine when she could heal him herself…!

"Cause, I can't. At least, not the old age stuff, never could. I can only take away some of the pain. …I'm going to bed… school tomorrow."

Hope said softly, "Okay."

Jeff said, "She read my mind like we were having a casual conversation!"

"I saw. Are her abilities growing?"

"I don't know, I guess we need to find out."

"No time like the present."

Jeff opened the back door and called out, "Megan…can you come here a minute."

Megan's muffled voice screamed! Clive stepped out with Megan. Her hands were tied, and her mouth was gagged. Clive had a gun to her head.

Instant rage, "What do you think you're doing?"

"I'm taking her and this time you won't find her."

"Do you honestly believe that?"

"Yes, I do. Because if you try to stop me, I will shoot you where you stand."

Megan gave Jeff a little nod.

Jeff raised his hands in surrender. "Okay, we won't stop you…"

Hope was horrified. "You can't let him go!"

"I don't see a choice, Hope. Mark my words I will tear you apart if anything happens to her,"

Clive laughed and dragged Megan toward the door. Hope made a move to go after them. Jeff stopped her. He whispered, "Stay back."

Suddenly realizing what was going to happen, she ducked behind Jeff and closed her eyes.

Clive shoved Megan out first and went to grab her arm. Haze struck first, ripping his heel. The instant he let go of Megan, Mazey jumped his back and knocked him down.

Jeff came out holding a gun pointing at Clive's head. "Mazey hold him there until I tell you to let him up. Clive, as much as I want to put a bullet in your head, I can't. Unlike you, I respect life."

"Let me up…"

"Sorry, you get up and they will rip you apart."

"Okay, let me go…I swear I'll never come back, never!"

"I don't believe you…"

"I promise…"

"Tell that to the police, they're on their way."

"Mazey; all of you leave quickly!"

They left and Hope brought out a broom and swept the wolf footprints away.

"Can I turn over now?"

"No…"

Police sirens could be heard off in the distance.

Clive spat, "Your life is over."

Jeff smiled, "How do you figure?"

"They will take Megan away and put her in foster care. You won't see her again!"

"Not hardly, we prepared for this. Hope is my wife and we adopted Megan."

Two squad cars pulled up. Sheriff Olson got out and sauntered over to Jeff and pulled out his gun. "You can stand down now, son."

"Thanks Uncle…"

"Is this the guy who's been creating all the trouble."

Jeff handed his uncle Clive's gun. "Yeah, his name is Clive Jenkins. He tried to kidnap Megan by gun point."

His uncle took the gun and shook his head. "Not smart, Mr. Jenkins."

Clive yelled, "They had the wolves attack me!"

"Wolves huh? Where are they?"

"I'm telling you they were here…"

"Sure okay, get up. Jackson take him into custody and read him his rights twice."

"Sure thing, Sheriff."

"And Jackson takes him to holding, I'll be along in a bit. I want to spend time with my nephew. I won't be long."

"Take your time, I got this."

Jeff hugged his uncle, "Come in, come in!"

Once they were seated, including Megan, the uncle said, "Okay, tell me the whole story."

For the next hour or so they told him almost everything. They left out Cumba and the wolves. He took notes all the way through their story.

"I'll say that's quite a story and this young lady with special powers is the cause. You, Missy, are a very important person. Tell me what it is you can do?"

Megan said firmly. "I can heal things and I will prove it!"

"How?"

Megan walked over to him and put both her hands on top of his head. She stood there for quite a while. Finally, she stepped back and said. "Your tumor is gone. You will be okay now."

"How did you know…"

"You kept thinking your head hurts and that it's going to get real bad cause the doctor said it would. Do you still have a headache?"

He blinked several times. "No, I don't, it's gone." His eyes filled with tears as he stared at Megan. "No wonder he wanted her! Hell, I want her!"

Jeff shocked by the diagnosis of the brain tumor asked, "Why didn't you tell me about this?"

"I didn't want the pitiful looks. You know the, I'm so sorry, it's annoying!"

"I understand." And he did understand. "When dad was sick, I didn't tell everyone, but I told you."

"Yes, and I will always be grateful. I guess with Anna gone, I didn't mind so much. I was looking forward to seeing her again."

Megan asked, "Do you want your tumor back?"

"Oh no Megan, not at all. I was just saying that if I was going to die it would be okay."

"One more thing," said Jeff. "We told Clive we were married and had adopted Megan, which is the plan. It just hasn't happened yet."

"I won't tell him any different. My advice, get that done before the trial. I've got to get back." He turned to Megan. "Thank you, young lady. I am truly grateful for the healing. Just be careful who's watching when you do it. There are more people like Clive out there, they just have different names."

She smiled, "Yes, sir. I'll be careful."

They all hugged each other with promises of more visits in the future.

"Well ladies, we need to get married! What do you say Hope, tomorrow?"

"Yes!" screamed Megan. "Okay Hope? Say yes, please."

Hope put her hands on her hips. "Well…of course! Tomorrow's fine!"

The two females ran into the house to make dinner. Jeff sat down on the porch relieved that for now the threat was over. He tried to relax but found it difficult. All of a sudden, he felt them coming, something he hadn't felt in many years, tears. He had no choice but to let them fall.

When Clive held Megan at gunpoint, the fear of losing them hit me so hard I was paralyzed with fear which made me vulnerable. That can't happen ever again. I need to control my fear, so I can protect them. And the realization that I led Clive here is more guilty than I can bear. I don't understand how he found us; I was extremely careful...

"Jeff dinner is ready..."

"Okay coming."

Chapter Twelve
The Wedding

The next morning, Jeff was awakened by two giggling females. He got up to find the coffee was made and poured himself a cup. When he finished and they still hadn't come out, he went to feed the animals.

Finally, the women left the bathroom. He barely had time to clean up before they had to leave. The hour and a half drive to the county seat felt like an eternity for Jeff. He glanced at Hope, she was absolutely perfect and Megan, although she brings us trouble, is too cute for words. His world was perfect, except for Megan's adoption. Without the proper paperwork, there is no way they will just let us keep her.

They had an appointment with Ms. Devon, later this afternoon, who said she would help us find a way to adopt Megan. The problem is that she wasn't in the system as an orphan. Hope never reported finding her nor filed paperwork to foster her. I'm afraid they will take her away until all the protocols are met and who knows how long that will take. If it wasn't for Clive's trial, Hope said she never would put Megan through any of this. I have to agree. It won't be that long until she's an adult, yes it will, she turns eleven soon.

Jeff pulled into the parking space. "We are early, which shouldn't be a problem."

"Good that will give us girls a chance to get changed."

Jeff wore his best pants and a sport jacket, that Hope ironed to perfection right down to the crease in the pants. What she was going to wear was a complete mystery. Whatever it was you can bet it was neatly folded inside the gunny sack she'd clinging to on her lap. Jeff smiled, *she could wear that gunny sack and she'd look beautiful.*

Jeff signed them in at the clerk's desk and took a seat. The name plate on the judge's pulpit said, the Honorable Greggory Hines.

"We have to change." Hope whispered to Jeff. "How much time do I have?"

"Twenty minutes, is that enough?"

She kissed him on the cheek and whispered, "It will have to be." She grabbed Megan's hand, and they fled back through the double doors.

There were several people ahead of them, so Jeff just watched the judge work. Some of the people were there for sentencing on petty crimes, a few on burglary and one guy for assault. Jeff was so engrossed that when the judge called his name, he didn't respond at first.

"Jeff Olsen…"

Jeff stood up, "Oh, sorry your honor. I'm here."

"And Hope? Is she here?"

"Yes, your honor. She is getting ready. Whatever that means."

"Awe, we've got time. You're the last case of the day."

"Thank you, I'll go and get them."

"No son. I've sent my wife to fetch them."

"Thank you."

"First time, son?"

"Yes, didn't realize it showed…."

"You're pacing."

Jeff stopped, "Yes, I guess I am. Didn't realize…."

"You'll be fine son. It seems that you waited a long time."

"My age gave me away?"

"Older than most."

A buzzer sounded. "Okay, here we go."

The double doors opened and in walked Hope holding Megan's hand. From the speakers the song started playing, Here Comes the Bride!

The judge came down from the pulpit to stand on the floor.

Jeff was stunned! Hope was ravishing in a white dress gathered at the waist, lace sleeves, and a lace vale across her face. She had pearls around her neck and ballet shoes on her feet. Her hair was pulled over to one side with spiral curls hanging down.

Jeff nearly cried; *she was so beautiful!*

The judge winked at Jeff. "She's a butte!"

"Yes, sir she is!"

"Okay son, are you ready?"

Jeff nodded.

"And who is this pretty young lady?"

"I'm Megan Hollis, sir and I'm going to be adopted! We are going to be a family once you put us altogether."

The judge smiled. "Okay, we better get started. Jeff and Hope will you step forward. Megan stands beside Hope. My wife Mary will stand up for you Jeff.

Megan nodded and Mary said, "I would be honored."

"Jeff, will you take Hope as your wedded wife? To have and to hold from this day forward…"

Megan couldn't concentrate on the ceremony as Mary looked like she was going to pass out. The instant she heard I pronounce you husband and wife! Megan ran to Mary and took her hands in hers. Mary was shocked and tried to pull away, but Megan hung on. Mary gave a shudder and her knees buckled. Jeff caught her on the way down to the floor and felt her neck, no pulse. Megan put her head on her chest and chanted.

The judge was trying to pull Megan away.

Jeff held him back. "Hope will explain what's happening."

Within a few minutes, Mary opened her eyes. "What happened?"

"You fainted," the judge told her, but kept his eyes on Megan. "Let's get you in the back to lay down for a while." She nodded. "You folks stick around you have paperwork to complete.

"Sure thing," said Jeff halfheartedly. Surely there's going to be a million questions.

The judge returned in short order. "You folks come to my chambers."

They followed him without question. Once settled, the judge looked directly at Megan. "Young lady, did you heal my wife?"

"Yes sir, I did. She was dying."

"Are you the young girl who Clive Jenkins tried to kidnap yesterday?"

"Yes, sir and another time too. Jeff and Hope rescued me from him."

"I suppose many people will try to kidnap you once they find out what you can do."

Jeff said, "Your honor, I am confident that Hope and I can protect her."

"You are? How? I understand he got into your house and held you all at gun point."

"I'm still trying to figure that out."

The judge picked up the phone and talked to someone for a minute then hung up. "I have an idea how. We'll have the answers in a minute."

He turned his attention back to Megan, "have you always been able to bring back the dead?"

"Yes…"

"What else can you do?"

Jeff stood up, "Please judge stop this…"

"I have something up my sleeve. Hang on son, I'll get to it in a minute. Answer the question Megan, please."

"I can talk to the animals and heal them too, I can hear and talk to ghosts like my dad, same with people's thoughts but only when they are upset."

"I see, I thought so." A lady came into the chambers carrying a bunch of papers and handed them to the judge. "Thanks, Clarice." She nodded and left. The judge was about to speak when an officer came in and handed him a gadget of some kind. The judge rolled it over and over in his hands. "I have an answer as to how he found you." He handed the object to Jeff.

Jeff looked at it, turning it over and back. "This is a tracking device of some sort, right?"

"Yes, highly sophisticated and newly developed."

"I didn't know they existed yet. I read about them just last week. How could they be out already?"

"This particular one is not a manufactured model, see there's no makers mark."

"Prototype?"

"That would be my guess, yes." The judge looked down at the papers in front of him and asked, "how can you two protect her? It is obvious that she is extraordinary!"

Megan stood up, "Mr. Judge, I don't need them to protect me! I have an army!"

"You do?"

"Yes sir, I do…" Megan looked at Jeff, he nodded. "We live on a big farm with tons of animals. All I have to do is call them to save me."

"We live about an hour and a half away. We could demonstrate. That's how Clive was caught, she called the animals. They pinned him to the ground until I got him tied up. They left when the sirens could be heard. We can demonstrate if you care to come out to our farm."

Hope said, "When I found her, she was living with wolves."

The judge's eyebrows went up. "Found her! Wolves?"

"Yes…"

"Megan is this true?"

Megan nodded, "Yes, Mazey found me and took me to their den cause the bad guys were getting too close."

The judge shook his head. "Mazey is a wolf and that's her name."

"They have names…!"

"So, you named them all?"

"Oh, no, the lead wolf names them at birth, cause he's the dad. All animals are named at birth just like us."

The judge was baffled but nodded his head in agreement. "Dogs too?"

"Yes…"

The judge pushed a button on his desk. The door opened and the lady who had brought the papers earlier poked her head in. "Clarice, bring in Roscoe please."

"Sure…" Within a minute, Clarice opened the door, and a black and tan Yorkie came bounding into the room.

Megan's eyes lit up. She got off the chair and sat on the floor. The dog immediately ran to her.

Hope was quietly explaining to the judge what was going to happen next. "She will mentally talk to him until he's comfortable hearing a human voice in his head. Then he will talk to her."

Megan looked up at the judge. "His birth name is Risky, but he doesn't mind Roscoe. Most animals hate their human names."

"Risky huh!" Risky started barking at the sound of his given name. "Amazing is all I can say." He paused before he began again. "This is what I want to do right now. I need to protect her, immediately. So, I'm signing an order to put Megan in your custody, temporarily until I can go to your farm. Let's say this Saturday at noon, will that be okay with you folks?"

"Yes, your honor. Are you saying that we do not have to go to the adoption agency?"

"All adoptions are finalized by me. I'm just alleviating the middleman. It's very important to me that the fewer people who know about her the safer she will be. If that's okay with you, we will continue our plans and I'll see you on Saturday."

"Saturday it is."

"Oh wait. Let's get the cheek swab done right now so we don't have to wait so long."

The judge swabbed Megan's cheek and sealed it in a plastic bag. He labeled it and called in Clarice again where he handed off the swab.

Jeff gave the judge their address and drew a detailed map to the farm. "Do I need to cancel our appointment with the adoption agency?"

"Already done son, get your family home."

On the way home, to celebrate their wedding day, Jeff took her and Megan to meet Hank and Alice at the feed store. They were in their thirties, a handsome couple. He had jet black hair and green eyes. Alice was stocky, blonde with beautiful blue eyes. They are kind-hearted people which drew Jeff to them instantly.

Those three women hit it off so well that Jeff invited them to dinner which they readily accepted.

Hank whispered to Jeff, "it's been a long time since Alice has had anyone to talk to besides me. I am grateful you brought Hope and Megan. Look at those women, giggling and laughing. I haven't seen Alice smile in years."

"I know Hope is happy look at her smiling too. Although she's never said anything, I know she's lonely at the farm. It's good for all of them." Jeff leaned in, "Chinese okay for you too?"

"Chang Ho's?"

"Yes…"

"Gosh I can't remember the last time we went out to dinner. Chang's is perfect! Let me see if I can get these women moving!"

Jeff walked outside. The day was perfect so far, but he felt doom looming. No, he chastised himself. I will not bring in doom and gloom, not today.

Megan and Hope chatted all the way to Chang's. When Hank parked the SUV, Hope looked up in surprise," We're here already?"

"Yes," replied Hank. "Good thing to, I'm starved."

Jeff was pretty sure that Hope had no idea where they were or what kind of restaurant they were at. Once they were seated, Hope finally looked around and noticed that the waiters and waitresses were Chinese.

Hope leaned in and whispered to Jeff, "Where are we?"

"Chang's!"

The waiter passed out menus to everyone. Hope took one look inside and realized that she had no clue as to what the names of the dishes meant. "I'm embarrassed, I've never been to a Chinese restaurant before."

Alice said softly. "This will be your new favorite food!"

Megan nearly as bewildered as Hope said, "Did we go to China, cause I wasn't looking where we were going?"

Jeff trying to keep a straight face by saying, "No, they came here to our country to make money. In their country, they cooked delicious foods which they now cook for us to enjoy."

"Wow!" Megan's eyes grew bigger by the minute as she contemplated how long of a journey that would be. "That's a long way to travel to cook us dinner!"

"That it is…how about you folks figure out what you want to eat. I'll be right back."

Hope was taken back by the abruptness in which he left, so she looked around and saw the man at Hank's SUV. "Megan, let's see if we can figure out the menu."

Megan snapped her head around to look out the window. She studied the man talking to Jeff and pointed, "That man was sent by Clive to hurt Jeff. Clive paid this man a lot of money to make sure Jeff will not be in court to testify. What does that mean, testify?"

"To tell the judge that he is a bad man."

"And he wants Jeff not to talk to the judge?"

"Yes…"

Megan frowned. "Clive is a bad man!"

"Yes, he is, and he will be locked up for many years. You don't need to worry, we will protect you, I promise."

Hank got up from the table and went back to the kitchen.

Alice was astonished that Megan obviously read that man's mind and maybe this is why Jeff has been so secretive lately.

"Hope, what do you do for a living?"

"I don't understand the question. But if you're asking me how I make money, then I would have to say, I garden, make preserves and pots and pots of soup. I take care of my husband and Megan. That's what I do, daily!"

"Oh Hope, I am so sorry! I was not attacking you, please don't take it that way."

"Sounded like you were challenging me and I'm not a harlot!"

"Oh no!" Alice started to cry softly. "I'm sorry…let me start over. Look, I work in a feed store and you?"

"I work at home…"

"Have you ever worked in a store or a dress shop?"

"Alice, I am or was Amish! In our culture, women are not allowed to work outside the home. Jeff is teaching me the way of your world and I admit, I've got a lot to learn! I'm sorry I made you cry. I didn't mean to."

"I had no idea you were Amish!" She smiled, "so that's how you know so much about food! And don't worry about the tears, I cry at the drop of a hat these days."

Megan giggled, "cause you're going to have a baby!"

"Who me? No…" Alice stopped and just stared at Megan. "Do you really think so?"

"You were sick this morning and the day before."

"How do you know that?"

She shrugged her shoulders. "I just know."

Jeff and Hank returned, Hank asked, "What's for dinner? Did you decide?"

"Sorry," Alice giggled. "We got to talking."

Megan announced, "Alice is going to have a baby!"

It was Hank's turn to stare at Megan, who couldn't stop smiling. "What is she talking about?"

Alice told him the events that led to the conclusion that she was pregnant. "Hank it all fits!"

It was obvious that it was Hank's turn to get teary eyed. "The more the merrier…"

Jeff and Hope teared up right along with them. "Well, that's two things to celebrate!"

"Two?" Hank asked. "What's the other?"

"Hope and I were married today!"

"Today!" exclaimed Alice. "We had no idea! Congratulations!

For their special occasions, Jeff ordered sparkling cider in lieu of champagne. They laughed a lot, but the highlight of the evening was watching Hope and Megan trying several different dishes.

"So much flavor!" remarked Hope. "They must use different oils and spices."

Alice swallowed a mouthful before she said, "I think it's called sesame oil and one of the spices is curry, I don't know the others. Oh wait, ginger root is another."

"Where do you buy them? Because I'd sure like to cook with them."

Hank said, "There's a Chinese market not far from here, I think it's over by where they have the farmers market in Hamilton,"

Megan, who had been quiet for quite a while, asked if Jeff could show her where the restroom was.

"Sure, come on."

They both rose and headed toward the kitchen. Once they were out of ear shot, Megan stopped Jeff.

"The man in that cab out front wants to kill you!"

"Megan please don't worry about him. I'm aware of what he's up to."

"No, he's put something on your truck, just like Clive did!"

"A tracker?"

"Yes, that's it..."

"Thanks Megan. I've got a surprise for him. Go to the bathroom."

Megan and Jeff returned to the table where Hope was all excited. "Is it true, we're spending the night here?"

"Yes! It is too late to drive home tonight, so I thought we could stay in my apartment which just so happens to be upstairs!"

A hundred chores ran through Hope's mind. The animals, night clothes, fresh clothes for tomorrow and the list kept growing.

"Whoa Hope, I can see your mind spinning. While you two giggly girls were in the bathroom this morning, I gathered enough stuff to keep us comfortable for one night."

"You did?"

"Yes, I did!"

Alice's eyes lit up, "Megan, would you come to our farm tonight? I have some very different animals for you to see…"

"Like what."

"We have emu's and a couple of alpacas."

"I've never seen those! Can I go with them, can I?"

"Are you sure Megan?"

"Yes, no one can find me at their house."

True, thought Hope. "Okay then, you can go. I'll get your things for tonight. I'll be right back."

Hank got up with Jeff and they both left. As soon as they got outside Jeff scouted the parking lot and the surrounding streets that he could see. "There's a tracker on my truck…"

"No," Hank smiled. "I put it on Frank's delivery truck! That ought to keep him busy for a while…"

"Thanks."

"You will need to tell me the story tomorrow."

"I will, I promise. How about you and Alice come out to our farm tomorrow, your store is closed?"

"Deal. Let's get moving before he finds out he's been duped."

In minutes, Hank, Alice and Megan were back in the SUV, and pulling out of the parking lot. Jeff and Hope climbed the stairs, excited about their wedding night. That's when the first shot rang out.

Megan screamed, "Jeff's in trouble! Go back!"

Hank swung the car around and headed for Jeff's apartment. Alice quietly opened the glove compartment and slid out the .357 Magnum which she put in Hank's lap.

Another shot rang out! Megan screamed, "Stop the car!"

"I have to get closer, Megan."

"If you pull in the parking lot, he will kill you. We are close enough now to get against the building."

Megan leapt out of the car the instant it stopped. She repeats under her breath, "only for good, only for good…"

She ran around the corner heading for the stairs. Megan screamed, "No, no, no, they're hurt!"

Hank picked her up around the waist and lifted her off her feet. "Megan what are you doing?"

"I can heal them! Let me go!" She struggled. "Please let me help them, please…"

Hank set her down. "You stay behind me, understood?"

"Yes! Just get me there hurry!" Sirens could be heard closing in. "No time, I have to get to them."

She took off like a shot and ran up the stairs. She grabbed one of Hope's hands and then one of Jeff's. No heartbeat! Jeff's dead! She let go of Hope's hand and buried her face in Jeff's chest. She began to chant. Squad cars were pulling in, she only had seconds before they'd pull her off of him. She closed her eyes and sent a jolt of electricity through him. He opened his eyes and gasped for air.

"You healed me, didn't you?"

She nodded and turned to Hope, who was moaning. She had a bad gash on her forehead from Jeff shoving her down.

She whispered to Jeff, "She'll be fine. You saved her!"

As predicted, the paramedics made her leave Jeff's side. Hank took her over to Alice. "I'm going to check on Hope first, then Jeff. Stay here with Alice, please."

Megan heard a man screaming not far away. The police took out on foot toward the screaming man. Megan smiled, *Mako found him*!

Alice saw her smile. Oh, my lord, she knows something about this! But before she could ask her, Hank was coming back with Hope. Megan ran to her.

"Hope and Megan are going to stay with us tonight. The paramedics said she needs looking after. Jeff will be in the hospital for a few days."

"Of course, I was going to suggest that myself!"

Hope whispered, "Jeff said he brought us overnight bags. I'm guessing they're still in the truck at your store." She began to cry.

"Alice, get her in the car, she looks like she's about to drop."

"You get their overnight bags, hurry please."

Hank got the overnight bags and put them in the back of his SUV. Deciding he better make sure it was okay to take Megan and Hope away from the scene, he stopped an officer to ask permission. The officer said it was okay as long as they had an address where she could be contacted. Hank gave him their address and phone number.

As Hank started back out the SUV, he heard, "Holy shit, the guy was mauled by wolves. We shot at them but missed!"

Hank got into the car and left the parking lot. He was relatively sure that man's death had something to do with Jeff. *I better get them to safety immediately because I don't know how many more shooters are out there.*

Once they got to the house, Alice fussed over them. She got blankets to cover them up with as they were shivering more from trauma than from the cold. Megan would not let go of Hope and in a few minutes began to softly cry. Unbeknownst to Megan, her tears soaked through Hope's shirt and healed the deep wound on her forehead and all the scratches from her being pushed down on the stairs.

"I almost forgot," said Hank. "The police want her dress, as it might have DNA transfer on it. They gave me a bag to put it in and it's in the car." He went out back and froze in his tracks, he had two flat tires! He called the police. It wasn't but two minutes before a squad car pulled up.

Hank walked around the side of the house and motioned for them to come back. They were the same officers from Jeff's scene. The one he knew was Officer Mead.

He explained that he had just come home from the scene and remembered the evidence bag for Megan's dress. That's when he found the tires.

"You've been home what ten minutes?"

"Yes, about that…"

"Did you go near the car?"

"No, sir. It shook me, after what happened to my friend! I immediately call you!"

"Okay, if you'll get me her dress, then get back in the house. I'm going to bring in the dogs."

"Yes, sir."

Alice was ready with the dress at the back door. "What's going on?"

"I'll tell you in a minute. Go back inside, please." She nodded. Hank turned and handed the dress to the officer.

"Now go back inside. I'll be back to talk to you." He walked a little farther into the yard looking around the ground. He bent over and picked up something off the ground and turned the object over and over in his hand. It was an AA thirty-day sober chip. He yanked open his phone, dialed and talked to someone on the other end of the line.

Mead knocked on the back door. "I'm pretty sure I know who did this to you. So, I'm not gonna bring in the dogs just yet. If it's not him, I may be back."

"When you find out for sure, will you let me know? And I'd like to know why!"

"I'll be in touch." He strode back to his police car.

Inside the house, Megan was in pajamas and sipping a hot chocolate. Hope had a cup of black coffee.

Hope said, "I want to explain to you what you saw Megan do." Hank and Alice both leaned forward in their chairs. "Megan can bring back the dead…"

Hank acknowledged, "I know, I watched her. Hope, Jeff was dead."

"That's why Clive wants her so badly! He's already kidnapped her once and we were grateful to get her back. He made a second attempt at our house yesterday! He was held for the police by Megan's wolves!"

Hank's mind started turning, "I saw that story this morning on the news! That was you?"

"Yes," said Hope. "But what has me confused is, why are they still coming after her?"

Alice asked, "he's behind bars, isn't he? So, who is after her now?"

"Clive can't exploit her from prison, but someone else could!" Hope thought out loud. "Maybe, he told someone else about her abilities and now he wants to use her."

Hank shifted in his chair. "I'll put sleeping beauty to bed."

Megan didn't move when Hank picked her up.

"She's exhausted poor thing. It was an exciting day for you both. Do you know how she's able to heal people?"

"No all she says, is that she only knows she can. Same with the animals she talks to…she hears their thoughts, and they hear hers."

"Wow! One small child can do all that!"

"The odd thing is, I think she can do much more. I'm sure she talks to ghosts, too!"

Hank returned and had been quiet throughout Hope's explanation. "Is Megan your daughter?"

"No, Jeff and I hope to adopt her." Hope started to cry.

"Enough interrogation for tonight, you are wiped out. Let me change your bandage and then you go to bed."

Alice went into the bathroom and got medical supplies. She sat across from Hope and started removing the bandage. When she removed it there was nothing there, no cut, no bump, nothing!

"I guess you won't need these! Why am I surprised that you're healed?"

The phone rang, Hank got up to answer it.

"Hank," it was Jeff. "Can you take them home right now?"

"Megan's asleep, but yes, we can."

"Hurry Hank, oh man, I'm sorry I've got you in the middle of this!"

"Don't worry it's not a problem."

"Yes, it is, but thank you. Can you guys stay with them tonight?"

"Yes…"

"Thank…." Jeff abruptly hung up!

"Let's go, now!"

Hank picked up Megan, while the woman grab the overnight bag then ran for the car. Hope gave Hank directions.

Hope blurted, "Tracker! Do we know if there is one on this car?"

"This car was in the barn, I just brought it up to the house today. But I think I'd better check."

After finding a machine shop, gas station combo that was open late, Hank jacked up one side, so he took a good look under the car. Nothing, but he decided to open the hood. There it was sitting right next to the radiator. He took it off and stuck it on a long-haul fuel truck that filled the station's fuel tanks. He hopped back into the car and took off.

"Good catch, Hope!"

"Thanks...how did Jeff sound?"

"Worried about you and Megan. I'm surprised the hospital hasn't called you."

"They can't I've never owned a phone, nor would I know how to use one..."

"Seriously?"

"Yes, Hank I am or was Amish!"

"I didn't get a chance to tell him, Hope. I'm sorry..."

"Alice, please don't worry about that. I need to fill you in on our farm and the animals we have."

Hope spent the whole ride home explaining about Cumba's and the Mazey's stories. The one story she had the most trouble telling was how she found Megan and Loki on the side of the road.

"That poor child!" Alice was nearly in tears, herself.

"After I heard her story, by keeping her, I knew what I was getting into. Just not Jeff and now you! This is all my fault..." Hope cried softly. "Hank, turn left into the next driveway. I have to get out to open the gate."

Hank hopped out, "I've got it Hope."

Once everyone was settled at the kitchen table, Hope offered coffee or wine.

"Wine!" Said Hank.

"Do you have juice or cold water?"

"Of course…" Hope poured her a glass of fresh squeezed orange juice.

There was a scratch on the door. Hope opened it and Cumba is standing there. "Oh shoot! I've got to feed the animals. Please sit and enjoy your drinks. It won't take me long."

"We can help!"

"If you're sure…I'd love the help."

In a matter of thirty minutes, all the animals were fed. When they returned to the house, Hope were surprised to see Loki sitting in the kitchen. "Something wrong, boy?"

Loki whimpered.

"Go see Megan, she can help you."

He went down the hall and entered the room. When he didn't come out after a while, Hope went to the door and peeked in. Megan had gotten out of bed and was curled up with Loki on the floor. She had her arm draped over his neck and her leg over his hindquarters.

The scene was heartwarming, and Hope whispered, "You're a good boy Loki."

Hope told them to go and peek, but don't step into the room.

Hank said, when they returned to the table, "If only people could see this! Maybe, they wouldn't be so frightened."

Alice had teary eyes. "Absolutely beautiful!"

They sipped their drinks in silence, each one lost in their own thoughts. Hank was the first one to break the silence. "Hope, you and Jeff have built a piece of heaven out here!"

"That is the way we look at it too, but I don't know how we are going to keep it that way. We need to find a way to end this mess and still keep our anonymity."

"Tall order, Hope."

"I know, Hank. There has to be a solution, there just has to be. I'm tired, I'll see you in the morning. Please make yourselves at home."

"Good night. We're going to turn in too."

Early the next morning, Jeff arrived home with his brother, Daniel. Hearing a strange male voice in the kitchen, Hope came flying out of the bedroom with a shotgun! Jeff and Daniel instantly put their hands up in surrender.

"Jeff!" Screamed Hope and put the shotgun down against the wall. "I'm so sorry!" She ran to him, and he scooped her up in his arms.

"It's okay honey…we have company. Meet my brother Daniel!"

"Daniel, hi! Nice to meet you…um, sorry about the shotgun."

"Don't worry, I would have done the same thing. But the shotgun doesn't scare me as much as that wolf!"

"Loki! He's a friend. It's okay!"

Loki stopped growling but didn't move or take his eyes off Daniel.

Jeff looked passed Hope and saw Alice and Hank standing in the hallway, but not Megan. "Hope can you wake up Megan?"

"Sure…"

Megan appeared, rubbing sleepy eyes. "Jeff!" She ran to him, and he dropped to one knee. She hugged him so tight; he almost lost his breath. "You're okay!"

"Yes, thanks to you, I need your help with Loki. But first meet my brother Daniel."

"Hi…" she said shyly.

"Hi…" he replied.

"Loki needs to feel that you are safe with my brother here. Would you make the introductions?"

"I can't, Loki decides. But I can ask him if there is a problem…"

"Yes please."

Megan went over to Loki, who was still fixated on Daniel. "Loki, what do you see?"

Death, death…

Show me…a picture formed. Daniel is falling to the ground. Megan jumped up and went to Daniel.

"Are you sick?"

His eyes filled with tears, he nodded.

Jeff was shocked and went to say, why didn't you tell me, but Megan stopped him.

"What type of sickness?"

"Pancreatic cancer…"

She looked up at Jeff. "I haven't cured sickness, but I will try?"

Jeff nodded, "Do your best. That's all anyone can ask for, okay."

Megan nodded, "Lay down please." Daniel complied.

Hope watched Megan go into a glassy-eyed trace while she lowered herself to the floor beside him. Hope thought she'd seen that confused look before but wasn't sure.

Megan buried her head in his chest and the chanting began so softly that no one could hear the words. In seconds, she lifted her head. "I can't heal him; cause I can't see where the hurt is!"

"It's okay, Megan at least you tried."

"No …if I could see it, I could cure it."

Daniel asked, "Would an x-ray work?"

Megan shrugged her shoulders. "I don't know what an x-ray is."

"Jeff, I picked up my X-rays before I got you out of the hospital. They're behind the driver's seat."

Jeff left the house and came back with an over-sized Manila envelope. He pulled one of the X-rays out and held it up to the light. "Look Megan, see these white areas? That's cancer. They put in a dye to light them, so the affected area can be seen. Does that help?"

Megan took the X-ray and sat down at the table. She turned it in all directions and kept looking at Daniel on the floor. Finally, she got up and knelt down, putting the X-ray across David's chest. Instead of her hands being balled up in a fist, she laid her hands flat where it showed cancer. Burying her face in his chest, she began a different chant and continued for several minutes.

"I don't know if it worked or not, but I think so. You would need to have another X-ray to see the results."

"Thanks for trying and I'll let you know what the doc says. But I do feel much better!"

"Breakfast anyone?" Hope called out. "I'm cooking!"

Alice called out, "I'll help!"

Chapter Thirteen
The Judge

The following Friday morning, Jeff told Hope and Megan that Stanley died, and he'd like to take Cumba back to the zoo.

"Yes please!" squealed Megan. "He's missing his friends.!"

Jeff was stunned! He thought Megan would throw a fit if he took the gentle lion away!

"Oh no…he is sad most of the time. He doesn't have long to live, and his friends would comfort him. That's what lions do."

"Okay, I will take him this morning." He smiled at Megan. "Second order of business is the judge is coming tomorrow and we need to be ready."

Hope laid her hand on his arm. "We are ready."

"We are?"

"Yes, we are. Yesterday, Megan and I cleaned all the pens, the house, and pulled the weeds. I've made soup for lunch with fresh bread. We are fine."

"What would I do without you?"

"Let's hope you never have to find out…look Jeff, Megan's rolling her eyes again. How about you go and tell Cumba that he's going home!"

She bolted out of the house and ran for the barn.

Very early the next morning, Jeff went out to his truck and to his surprise Cumba was in his crate in the back. "Did you get him back there?"

"Well sort of, I healed his joints enough in his feet, legs, and his hips which let him climb up there by himself."

"Nice work! We'll be leaving now."

Hope and Megan waved goodbye to their beloved friend, Cumba. They knew that it was best for him to be back with his friends, but it was hard on the heart.

Megan was softly crying, "I'm going to miss him so much…"

"Me too Megan, me too. Let's finish the laundry, I don't want the judge to see our undies waving in the breeze!"

Megan laughed through her tears, "No…we wouldn't."

Two hours later, Jeff's truck pulled into the barn. He wasn't sure that someone wasn't still after him. Even though the trial was still a long way off, he was sure Clive would keep trying to keep him from testifying. He shook all the annoying thoughts about Clive away. He brought home a surprise for Hope and Megan.

When he came in the back door, he had a big grin on his face. Hope instantly noticed that he had a basket of laundry. Probably from the zoo, she thought until the basket whimpered.

"Jeff! What do you have in there?"

She went to take the basket from him, he swung it out of reach.

"Jeff, what is in the basket?"

"It's for Megan too. Where is she?"

"Folding clothes…I'll get her."

Jeff put the basket down on the table while he waited for the girls to come out of the bedroom. He hoped this present would cheer up Megan and Hope too.

Megan came bounding out of bedroom, "You have a surprise for us? Me *and* Hope!"

"Yes…but I'm not sure you're going to like it. But Cumba thought you might be sad with him gone so he sent me home with these." Jeff took off the cover of the basket.

Hope and Megan peered into the basket and found two baby tigers.

"Tigers!" Hope reached the basket to pick up one of the cubs.

"Real Tigers?" squealed Megan.

"Yes, real tigers!" He couldn't help getting caught up in Megan's enthusiasm.

"And Cumba sent them?"

"He brought them to me himself."

"I did talk to him about tigers, a long time ago. I told him that I'd probably would never see one."

"Well, he must have remembered!"

"Tell him thank you for me. Just say it, he will understand."

"Okay I will, I promise."

Hope began making bottles, filling them with goats' milk she had in the refrigerator. "Jeff, do we have two large baskets so I can make a cave. I'll need wire too."

"Yes, do you want plastic or wicker?"

"Wicker…"

"I'll be right back." Jeff ran for the barn.

"What do you think, Megan?"

"I think they are amazing! And beautiful! And wonderful!"

"And, perhaps, they need us to take care of them…."

Megan readily said, "Yes, definitely!"

"How about we feed these little guys so I can make dinner for us."

"I can feed them by myself."

"Okay, then I'll start dinner, but first let me warm up these bottles. They are too cold for their tiny tummies."

Megan was in heaven with her tiny charges. There is no doubt in Hope's mind that they will not lack a single thing.

Jeff came in with two very large wicker baskets. After wiring the top to the bottom, he filled the bottom with straw from Cumba's bed and lastly, the smelly worn clothes from the zoo finished the cave effect. *It was perfect*, thought Hope and she hugged him tightly.

"Dinner's ready," Hope said loudly. Megan opened her door and came to the table. "Are they sleeping?"

"No…they are looking for their mom."

"What about the stuffed bear we used for Haze?"

"Um, Haze tore him apart when she was getting new teeth…"

"Awe, so do we have anything fuzzy we could use?"

Jeff said, "How about those fuzzy socks you bought me, Hope? Will they work?"

Hope folded her arms, "So, Jeff, am I to assume you don't like the fuzzy socks?"

"I wear those socks at night all the time. They keep my feet warm!"

"Jeff, are you willing to donate those precious socks to the cubs?"

Jeff winked at Megan, "Yes, of course, I am!"

Megan was giggling. Hope was trying not to. "So, might you know where these socks are located?"

"Um…, well, maybe I used them for Cumba's cold feet. He really needed them!"

Hope and Megan both laughed out loud. Hope asked, "Are they in the barn?"

Jeff headed for the door and crossed his fingers that they were in one piece.

"Hope…," said Megan softly. "These babies don't have names."

"No! I wonder why?"

"The dad was not there when they were born…"

"How about you give them names?"

"Can I really?"

"Sure….!" Hope smiled at her excitement.

"I know!" exclaimed Megan.

"What?"

"Tick for the boy and Tock for the girl!"

"Very clever, Megan!"

Megan beamed and ran to her bedroom where the cubs slept.

Jeff returned without the socks. "I'll go to the feed store tomorrow and get something fuzzy there."

"Okay we better eat and then get some rest for our big day tomorrow.

Hope got up early and found that Megan was not in her room. She went to the kitchen window and peered out. she found Megan expressing the Cubs. *I'm pretty sure she's gonna make the best mom ever.*

An hour before the judge was due to arrive, Jeff, Hope, and Megan did a last-minute inspection of the farm. Jeff's nerves were beyond raw. He woke up with a sour stomach but chocked it off to anxiety. It's not every day a man gains a family and Megan completes the picture.

A car could be heard coming up the road, and Jeff was sure that it was the judge as not many cars came up this far from town. When he knocked on the door, Hope let him in and offered him a seat at the table. Jeff and Megan were already seated.

The judge looked at Megan and smiled. "So, Megan… any new critters?"

"Yes, two baby tigers! You want to see them?"

"Of course, I would?"

Megan ran to her bedroom and emerged with the wicker den. Jeff walked over and took the den from Megan as it was awkward for her to carry. He set it on the table, where she instantly reached inside and pulled out a cub.

She handed the first cub to the judge. "This one is Tick, he's the boy." The next one she pulled out, she kept. "This one is Tock; she is a girl!"

The judge was enthralled by holding the baby tigers but put them back in the den. "Beautiful Megan."

"Thank you…but I have to take them outside now, cause I woke them up."

"Okay…we will wait to talk until you get back."

"I'll only be a minute…"

The judge nodded and went to the front door, once he opened it, he waved for someone to come in. "My stenographer Anna, she has to document our conversation."

With the cubs put away, Megan sat down on Hope's lap. Once she was settled safely in Hope's arms, she looked up and locked eyes with the judge. "He's not here to help me, he's here to take me away!"

Jeff stepped forward. "Judge is that true?"

"Let me explain, please…"

Megan got up and hid behind Jeff. "He has officers outside ready to take me! I'm not going!"

The judge, although shocked Megan read his mind, held up his hands in surrender. "If you're not going to listen, this meeting is over. Anna bring in the officers."

"Okay…okay, we'll listen!" Jeff returned Megan to Hope. "Tell us what we need to know."

"Remember the DNA test we took in my office?" They nodded. "Well in doing our background check her biological mother showed up. And we are obligated to notify her that her daughter is going to be adopted."

Megan felt a tug on her shirt. "My dad is here, just so you know."

"She can request to be reinstated as her parent or sign away all rights."

"My dad says she did sign away her rights and he can prove it."

"How?" The judge wanted to know. A key appeared on the table in front of the judge. His eyes widened, but he kept a level head. "What's this?"

"My dad says that key is for a safety deposit box at Four Corners Bank, 328 is the box number. Everything you need to know is in that box."

"I promise you I will check this out. But, in the meantime you do have to come with me."

"NO!" screamed Megan. "You don't understand! I'm not going with you!"

The judge hung his head and was quiet for a minute or two. "Megan, I'd like to make a deal with you, okay?"

Hope turned Megan around so they were face-to-face. "I see that angry look and I'm asking you to not do anything that will take you away from us forever. Do you understand?"

Her face softened, "Yes, only for good, right?"

"Yes, only for good. Let's listen to him first, please…"

"Okay…. but I don't want to leave you, please don't make me leave."

"I want you with us forever, you do know that right?"

Megan nodded. Hope turned to the judge, "Say your piece judge and make it quick!"

"I knew Megan would have this reaction. Hell, what child wouldn't. I cannot put her in foster care, due to the threats against her. So, if it's okay, Megan, I'll take you home with me. Mary would love to have you visit…and, I have guards that will make sure you're safe. This arrangement is just until we sort all of this out, I promise. What do you think?"

"That does sound pretty good, Megan….," said Jeff. "I know that means you have to leave us, but it will only be for a short time."

Megan looked at the judge, "Do you have animals other than Risky?"

"Actually, I do! I have two baby African Gray parrots. Mary is teaching them to talk! It would be nice if you could tell us their names!"

Megan understood by reading his mind that she had to go with him. It was the law; the judge was not being mean. "Okay, I will go." She came out from behind Jeff and headed to her room.

No one spoke until Megan returned with her suitcase.

The judge stood and looked directly in their eyes. "I swear as a District Court Judge, that I will investigate this matter fully. I'm taking this key with me to help figure this out. Is that alright with you?"

The judge felt a tug on his shirt and immediately looked all around him. He looked at Megan and she was smiling! "Your dad I suppose?"

"Yes sir. He won't hurt you; I promise."

"I didn't feel threatened at all. In fact, I felt reassured that there is an afterlife. Thank you for that validation."

Tug!

"He says you're welcome."

Jeff was proud how well they held up as the judge took Megan out to his car. However, the instant the car pulled away, Hope lost it. All he could do was hold her, while his own tears spilled over. It took a while before they could get themselves under control.

"Jeff let's get out of here. How about Chinese?"

"Jeff grabbed his coat. "Good idea! I'll grab the cubs if you'll get their bottles."

As they sped toward town, Hope cuddled the cubs, no doubt for comfort. "How are we supposed to go back to an empty house?"

"It's not empty. We have all our animals. Speaking of which, I'm going to take the cubs to the zoo. Kathy said she'd watch over the cubs while we eat and if you're up to it, we could visit Mary and Hank."

"Sure, I'd like that." She teared up, again. "Would you mind staying in town tonight too?"

"You're in luck. My apartment is still mine for the next two days!"

More tears, so Jeff reached over and held her hand. "It will be alright, Hope."

She nodded and tried to stop crying.

They were nearing Flatbottom Lake. "Hope, where do want to go first?"

She whispered, "Hank's and Mary's...." The cubs were starting to whine softly. Laying them across her lap on their backs, she pulled two bottles out of the bag and began to feed them. Her lap was nearly too small for the rapidly growing cubs. Then what? Well, she thought, that conundrum would have to wait for another day.

Jeff pulled into the zoo's parking lot, and they got out. Jeff took the cubs and Hope carried the bag with their bottles. Kathy, a pale woman in her mid-fifties, dressed in coveralls was waiting for them. She took the bag from Hope.

"Follow me, please. I made a small enclosure, it's all ready for them."

"Thanks Kathy.... you're the best."

"Thank you, boss. I'll put these bottles in the fridge in a minute. Have they eaten recently?"

"Yes," said Hope. "I just finished feeding them."

"Great!"

Jeff asked, "Any news on what's going to happen with the zoo?"

"Tons of rumors of course, but the scuttlebutt is that the land is being sold and these animals are going to be moved to the Pittsburg Zoo."

"That makes the most sense, I suppose."

"Here's the enclosure," she opened the door to the most incredible playpen for the cubs!

"Kathy, this is amazing! They are going to have a field day playing in this! Did you design this?"

"Yes...."

"Heck, I want to play here!"

"Thank you…" She was blushing now. "I like designing spaces for animals."

"You should start a business doing just that! People would pay good money to know their pets were happy."

"Maybe… I'll get the chance to think about your idea after we close this place."

Jeff and Hope left the zoo and headed to Flatbush. It was obvious that Kathy put Hope in a better mood. She went on and on about how amazing the enclosure was perfect for the cubs, etc. Jeff smiled for the first time today.

The feed store was crowded. It must be a shopping day! Hank waved as they came in and Alice had a line at the register that wound around the chicken feed aisle twice.

Hope ran to the register and started bagging people's purchases. Jeff went and helped Hank lug hundred-pound feed sacks to the loading dock.

"What the heck Hank! You got a two for one sale going on here?"

"No, I don't have a clue why we are so busy! Never happened before."

"Looks like the whole county is here. Maybe, they know something we don't?"

"Maybe…. I'm not complaining."

Jeff chuckled, "I wouldn't either."

After an hour or so, the crowd dwindled to nothing, and they all breathed a sigh of relief. It was way passed closing time. Hank closed the door and locked it. He did the same with the loading dock.

Alice made a pot of coffee and they all sat down on bales of hay.

"Hey thanks man for the help. I was getting wore out."

"Not a problem, Hank. Glad to help."

"What brings you here?"

"We came to take you to dinner."

"You better say Chinese, because I'm starved…."

"I am…is that okay with you Alice?"

"Most definitely! Let me put these cups away and turn off the pot."

At Chang's there was very little talking. Everyone had a mouth full of food and the only escaping sound was 'yum and oh, and this tastes so good'.

Once the plates were taken away, Alice stopped and looked at Hope and Jeff. "Where is Megan?"

Jeff did the explaining, "We're going to stay upstairs tonight. We just can't be home right now."

Hank looked at Alice and she nodded, "We would appreciate it if you stayed with us, because I'm sure you didn't bring anything with you."

"You're right we didn't."

"We have sundries and clothes at the feed store, plus fresh coffee, okay?"

"We thank you," said Jeff.

"Let's go…"

By the time they returned from the feed store, it was time for the ten o'clock news.

The living room looked like a pajama party as Hank turned on the television and found the news channel.

Hank sat next to Alice and said, "Maybe we'll find out why the store was so crowded."

"Maybe...." Jeff said, as he sipped his coffee and grabbed a fist full of popcorn.

"This is your 10 o'clock news and I'm Jack Burger! First, we have 'Breaking News' out of the Midwest. All the states are reporting record rains. Which means the drought is over, however with the exorbitant amount of rain creates rapid new growth. Now there is an upsurge of locusts. They are eating their way across the fields. Expect higher prices this year especially for baked goods, corn, and corn products. Basically, all ground crops."

"When we come back from the commercial break, I have, just in, a Jail Break in Haynes!"

Jeff and Hope sat upright and stared at the television. Each was afraid to speak until the newscaster came back on.

"This is stupid...I'm just being paranoid," said Jeff and leaned back. "Not every escapee is going to be Clive..."

"You're right...." muttered Hope, but her stomach did a little flip, and her first thought instantly ran to Megan's safety. He's found her everywhere we went, and if he was free, this time wouldn't be any different.

Hope was so lost in thought, that she didn't notice the newscaster had returned. All of a sudden, Jeff grabbed her hand and squeezed.

"Noooo," Jeff bellowed. "I need to call the judge!"

Hank pointed to the wall in the kitchen. "Help yourself...."

"Thanks...." Jeff dialed the number and hoped the judge was not asleep. But a very sleepy voice answered the phone. "Judge I am so sorry to wake you, but Clive has escaped."

"What!"

"The Hayne's County sheriff was transporting several prisoners to the jail for tomorrow's court and a semi-truck carrying a load of hay lost its brakes and plowed into the sheriff's van. All three prisoners escaped. Please make sure Megan is safe."

"Son, Megan is with her mother. The court gave her custody this morning."

"How is that possible? You just took her this morning!" Jeff started pacing. "Where does the mother live?"

"I'm sorry, I can't tell you."

"Can you tell me her name?"

"Sorry, no."

"Did you at least look at the information her dad gave you?"

"The court took it, they said they'd look at it, but they still gave the mother custody."

Jeff was defeated. "Thanks judge, sorry to wake you." Jeff hung up. He wanted to kick something and looked at Hope. She was softly crying.

Alice went over to console her, while Hank and Jeff went outside.

"This is incredible, Hank….and there is not one thing I can do to protect her…."

"True enough, but the one thing you haven't considered is Megan. She is a powerful little girl and I'm pretty sure you haven't seen a tenth of what she's capable of."

"You're right! And her dad will watch over her too. Thanks Hank, I was afraid I was going to lose it."

"It's been a rough night. How about a beer?"

"Yes, I think I will, thanks!"

Chapter Fourteen
The Hunt for Megan

Judge Hines, Mary and Megan entered the courtroom and sat in the first row. It would be fifteen minutes before the family court judge would begin proceedings.

Megan was surprised that the room was empty. "Where are all the people?"

"They'll be here shortly." The judge took Megan's hand. "I want to explain to you what is about to happen. Is that okay?"

"Yes, please...."

"Okay, remember when we took the cheek swab and the blood for the DNA test?" Megan nodded. "Well, we found a match for you in the data base."

"You did?"

"Yes. It was your biological mother. Do you understand?"

"I think so. The lady who gave birth to me."

"Yes. And she petitioned the court to give her custody of you. The judge will either grant or deny her request. I did give this judge all the paperwork that was in the bank's deposit box and he has a letter from Jeff and Hope and one from Hank and Alice."

Megan nodded. "Um, do I have a say in where I go?"

"No, I'm sorry."

***

Megan studied the woman, intently. This woman, Irene Cob, was not a happy person, she was dark and broody. Megan was quite sure she did not like this woman at all. But the judge said I had to give her a chance. After all, she *is* my mother. And there was no doubt that this woman is her mother. We look exactly alike, right down to the violet eyes. It was a bit creepy looking at someone who had the same face as you.

Oh, how I missed Hope and Jeff, she thought and made a promise to herself to find a way to get back home. As badly as she wanted to put a hex on this woman, she thought about what the judge told her. Do not expose your powers to anyone, unless you are positive, they won't exploit you. He had to explain to me what that meant.

"So young lady," Irene inquired, "does your name have meaning?"

"I don't know…"

"Ok, were you named after a family member?"

"I think Megan was my grandma's name."

"That's nice…" Irene paused. "I had a name picked out for you while you were in my tummy."

"You did! What was it?"

"Gypsy Rose…."

"That's a pretty name. thank you. Where are we going?" asked Megan.

"Oh here and there, no real direction."

"Like a vacation!"

"Sort of a working vacation."

"What kind of work?"

"You are going to heal people. I already have your first appointment in New Jersey."

So, she already knows. Megan's heart sank, and now *I work for her just like the judge said.*

"Can I put the seat back and take a nap."

"Sure kiddo…. we've got a long drive ahead."

"Thanks," she pulled the lever that released the back of the seat and pushed it down as far as it would go. With her back to Irene, she curled up in a ball and closed her eyes. Her heart hurt so bad that she called out with her mind, *Jeff, and Hope, I miss you so much!*

Alice and Hope were making a late breakfast. When all of a sudden, Megan's voice echoed around the room. "I miss you so much!"

Hope screamed, "We miss you too, baby. Where are you? Can you hear me?"

Jeff chimed in, "Megan, can you tell us where you are? Keep talking baby! What is that woman's name?"

Everyone paused in silence, hoping for another utterance from Megan.

Hope, in sheer frustration, cried out, "Will we ever find her?"

* * *

Clive could not imagine his good fortune, when he opened the trashcan lid and found oily jeans and a greasy plaid shirt. *These are perfect!* They looked to be two sizes too big. He scurried between the buildings and changed as quickly as he could.

Okay, he thought, *one problem down, several more to go.* Back to the trashcan, he buried the prison garb deep in the trash. He kept an eye out for a knit cap or floppy hat to hide his face. But more importantly, he needed big socks that would cover the wrist and ankle bracelets until he could find a way to get them off. It took many more trashcans before he scored a black knit cap and several pairs of stripped knee-socks.

I could cut the feet off to cover my handcuffs, he thought. All I'd need is something sharp to cut with, a knife or a pair of scissors would be best. He thought for a minute, people normally don't throw away knives or scissors, unless they are broken, so maybe an open toolshed? He looked up and down the alley. No doors were open, and he was terrified of leaving this row of houses, as they had become his safe haven. Taking his fingers, he rumpled his hair to look disheveled and put on the knit cap.

Not enough, he thought. Deciding that the only remaining problem was being recognized. My face needs to be altered. Grease would blur my facial features. There is an old wagon in the field at the end of the block. I can sneak down there tonight. Hopefully, there's still wet grease on the hubs.

Within three days, he had a complete disguise and was really pleased with himself that no one would believe that he was Clive Jenkins. Now he felt safe enough to venture out of his safe zone and walk around town, keeping to the outskirts and never meeting anyone eye to eye.

The next night on his rounds to get food from the café's throwaways, he heard several people talking really loudly at one of the outdoor café tables. They were all excited about a young girl, they heard about, that could heal any ailment. Rumor has it, that she even brought back a man that dropped dead in front of her.

Clive was shocked that people were talking about her two hundred miles north in the next county. Jeff and Hope were desperate to keep her abilities a secret. Something had drastically changed so he kept listening, hoping they would tell the whole story. However, the only thing he learned that a woman, named Irene, was going from town to town having Megan heal people for a hefty price. *Where's the next town… is what I want to know.*

He was about to move on, but another man joined them, and he repeated the story a second time. This time there was a little more information.

The guy became so engrossed in telling his story, he did ask one question. "Where are they headed? Do you have a phone number?"

"North   Carolina, I think and no phone number that I know of, sorry. Do you need help? Her kind of help?"

"No, how do I find them?"

"You could ask at the thrift store on 9th and Pioneer Street. I heard that's where she was...."

"Thanks...." He took off running towards 9th.

I need to follow him! I can listen to the questions he asks and maybe I can find out where she's going to next.

Clive skirted the alley in hopes of not being noticed. As he exits the alley onto Pioneer Street, he looked toward 9th and finds the guy reading what looks to be a flyer.

Throw it down! He thought.... *I need to read it too!* The guy just stood there looking at the flyer for a very long time. *What's he doing?*

Well, I could just walk by and see if I can read where she's going off the flyer, or I can just ask him. He decided on the latter.

"Excuse me sir. Is that a flyer about the healing lady?"

"Yes, it is."

"Does it say where she's going to next?"

"Yes, somewhere near Gainsboro, North Carolina."

"No address?"

"Just the Mills Mall Craft Center.... that's it."

"That's going to be hard to find.... damn it!"

"There is a small village to the south. I can't remember its name right now, but they are a crafting village. You know like small shops that sell handmade goods. Some sell fruits and vegetables. That would be a perfect place for that horrid woman to set up a booth."

Clive was taken back by the man's statement. "What do you mean?"

"My brother was in line waiting for his turn to see if she could fix his stomach, cancer. He will die soon. I wanted to see if she was real or not. I watched from across the street, and I noticed a few things. The poor girl looks like she's starving. Her eyes were sunken in her sockets and her hair was stringy, unhealthy looking. I swear that when they were packing up, she made the girl breakdown the whole booth by herself. She's such a tiny thing. Several men jumped in and helped her load the truck."

"Did she fix his stomach?"

"When she took his hands in her's, she smiled. I swear to you she glowed and then my brother cried like a baby. He says that all his pain is gone. Something, I'll never forget, that smile."

"That's wonderful. man…."

"Yes, it is and now she's gone, and I feel like a heel."

"Why?"

"I should have helped her somehow. She healed my brother, and I did nothing but watch that horrid woman mistreat her."

"Seriously, what could you have done? Anything that you tried to do would get you arrested?"

The man looked up from the flyer for the first time and stared at me for a full minute. "You're right. If I had laid one finger that woman, I would be in jail. Still, someone should step in and rescue that poor child."

The man handed me the flyer and walked off down the street. Clearly, he was upset over the treatment of Megan.

Clive was stunned. The Megan he knew would have fought tooth and nail to get away from anyone who mistreated her. So why not now? She must feel she has no choice but to stay. What happened that Jeff and Hope lost her? They fought so hard to keep her safe….so where are they? Something drastic has happened with no way for me to find out either. Ok…. I need to find Megan so I can see for myself what condition she's in.

For the next week, Clive hitchhiked across three states to get to Gainsboro only to find out that she left the night before. He scoured the area for an hour to find another flyer and found one tangled in the shrubs.

Well, let's see where she's headed to this time. Looks like Jax, Florida. Is that even a place? Seems so, okay, I've got to eat which means finding recyclables and then find a ride.

Since there was a huge crowd here to witness the girl's miracles, recyclables were easy to find. At least enough to get a hot meal and coffee. Now to find a ride, which proved to be quite difficult. On the back of her flyer, he wrote 'Bound for Jax, Florida', with a charcoal stick left over from an open fire and headed to the main road. He attached the sign to the suspenders on his back with the big safety pins he found a while back in the trash. He started walking on the shoulder in hopes that someone would stop and offer him a ride, just like always. After five hours of walking in the sun, no one stopped. Thirst from the warmer temperature was making him very uncomfortable, his dry throat hurt and the sweat that was running down his back had starting to itch. Not to mention hunger was creeping in again.

I need shelter and water, but the next town is still five hours away on foot. Well, I do see a barn up ahead which I'm sure has a loft and hopefully a water trough for the animals. That will have to do.

As he got closer to the barn, he was surprised that the farmhouse was nowhere to be seen. He peeked inside and indeed it had a loft with hay bales, but what excited him the most was the trough. It was ten feet in length, five feet wide and approximately four-and-a-half-feet tall. *I can bathe and wash my clothes!* Now he was grateful that he spent one whole afternoon draining shampoo bottles that people threw out on trash day. He drank from the trough, very careful not to stir up the sediment on the bottom. Although the water was warm, it felt cooler compared to the outside temperature. He kept a look out for people coming to the barn, so far no one showed up.

So, he found a bucket inside the barn just inside the door. Filling it up, he got out the bar of soap and wash cloth he stole in another town and began scrubbing his body. The warm water felt good on his skin and by using his tin cup to rinse his hair it fell in ringlets down his back. He felt like a new man.

Putting on his set of dry, clean clothes, he started washing the stinky set he took off. He finished just in time as it was dark and he was exhausted, and that loft looked really good for his tired legs. He picked up his wet clothes and put the bucket in the exact place where he found it, then climbed up into the loft. He moved a couple of bales to make room for a bedroll and draped the wet clothes over a bale of hay. Making a pillow out of loose hay, he fell asleep instantly.

Sometime during the night Clive woke up to the sound of loud music and a truck pulling into the barn.

Oh crap!

The truck pulled into the barn with the high beams on, the whole barn lit up like a roman candle.

Don't move, don't blink, because they will see me if I do! Just lay still and close your eyes.

Two doors slammed shut, two men.

One man said, "Greg would you climb up and throw down two bales. I'll turn the truck around and don't miss this time!"

"Sure thing! You know Dave, you could park closer…."

"Yeah! Yeah!"

The truck was repositioned under the loft and Greg grabbed the two bales closest to the ladder. Bang, bang, they both landed in the bed of the truck. One of them jumped into the bed and maneuvered the bales forward.

"Dave, did you see that healing girl?"

"Yes, very creepy if you ask me."

"I've known Harry my whole life and he's always been sickly. But when she laid her hands on him, you could actually see the healing running through him."

"What I saw was all the dough she was raking in, had to be thousands."

"You know Dave that could be us!"

"How do you figure?"

"Well, we could just snatch her up and run off with her. Put her on display and cash in too!"

"Well, I guess we could. We'd have to find her first though. And that could really be a chore since we don't know where she's going next."

"I do," Greg smirked and handed Dave a pint of whiskey.

"Thanks! What are you going to drink."

"I've got my own bottle!"

They both climbed into the bed of the truck and leaned against the bales. While they drank, they devised a hundred ways they could kidnap Megan and get away with it. Most of which included killing the woman. They also came up with a hundred ways to get rid of her body. They had unholy plans for Megan, too.

I've got to help her. Who knows how many others are thinking the same thing!

Two hours later and another round of pints, they passed out snoring like little truck drivers. Clive climbed down out of the loft and grabbed the hay hook off the wall. He slit both their throats and rolled them, and the hay bales out of the bed. With the bucket, he washed away all the blood. He went through all their pockets, took all the cash, and pulled the truck out of the barn. At least, these two won't be kidnapping anyone anytime soon.

He needed to get far away from here in case someone recognizes the truck. Once he had forty miles under his belt, he relaxed, and his heart stopped pounding. He was going to need gas soon and he needed a map of Florida.

The sun was coming up before he found a gas station that was open. He filled the truck and went inside to pay the clerk. That's when he spotted a phone on the wall.

"Excuse me, can I use this phone?"

"Sure, do you know the number?"

"Yes, but it's a Pennsylvania number…"

"I see…. That's a different procedure. Here I'll get it started for you." He took the phone and dialed 0. When the operator came on the clerk asked for time and charges for the phone call. "Here tell her the number."

Clive took the receiver and recited the number, the phone rang.

"Hank's Feed Store…."

"Hank this is Clive, I have news about Megan."

"Okay, tell me…."

"People are saying that the woman she's with is working her to the bone and Megan looks sickly. Someone needs to get her away from this woman. They are headed to Jax, Florida and I'm heading there now. I will call you back to give you details on her true condition. Oh, and people are getting the idea to kidnap her for themselves. I've permanently stopped two who were going to try in Jax." Clive hung up before Hank could say a word.

The phone rang and the clerk picked up the receiver, "Thanks operator." He turned to Clive and said, "Three bucks."

Clive paid him and then looked for something to eat. He turned and spotted a coffee pot. "Is this coffee for sale?"

"You got a cup or thermos?"

"No, where do I get those?"

Pointing to the other side of the store, "Isle three, over yonder."

I should get both, pretty clever this thermos is a must. Choosing the tin cup and a black thermos, he took it to the clerk who filled it with coffee. He also laid three sandwiches', a family size bag of chips, and a package of Fig Newtons on the counter. The clerk put it all in a paper bag and Clive asked, "Which way to Jax, Florida?"

"About a hundred twenty miles straight ahead. You'll see the signs."

Clive waved as he pulled away.

Chapter Fifteen
The Marketplace

Hank put the phone back in its cradle and yelled for Jeff.

"Be right there...."

Hank paced until Jeff appeared in the doorway. "Jeff, I just received a call about Megan!"

"Is she alright?"

"I don't think so...." He repeated the conversation leaving out the name of the caller.

Jeff paced around for a while shocked that he described Megan's condition as sickly. His anger grew as he thought about Irene, Megan's so-called mother. "Who called?"

"He said his name was Clive!"

"Clive! Are you sure?"

"Yes, it was him and he sounded genuinely concerned about her welfare."

"What can I do?"

"First things first, call the judge. See what he says."

"Good idea. I've got his number in my wallet. I'll go and get it." Jeff tore out of the store, like his boots were on fire. He returned waving the judge's phone number. "Got it! We were afraid this would happen to her. Damn it!"

Hank put a hand on Jeff's shoulder to help calm him and pulled him over to the customer's table. "Sit down a minute and gather yourself."

Jeff complied. He was shaking all over and couldn't put two words together.

"Stay here a minute. I'll be right back." All Jeff could do was nod. Hank ran to the cash register and opened the cabinet door underneath. Pulling out two glasses and a bottle of Jack Daniels, he headed back to Jeff. He poured a shot in each glass and handed one to him, "Drink this...."

Jeff grabbed the glass, threw his head back and swallowed. He let the whiskey burn all the way down his throat. Since he wasn't a drinker, it only took a minute for the whiskey to hit his head. He stopped shaking, but he still had a problem talking. He held out his empty glass for Hank to refill. This one did the trick, so he dialed the number.

The phone rang and was picked up immediately, the whiskey-voice said, "Judge Hines...."

"It's Jeff Olsen. I have news about Megan, and I need your help or advice on what I can do."

The judge's voice was suddenly tight in his throat, "She's working her, isn't she?"

"Yes sir, she is and from what I hear Megan looks horrible, well the exact word was sickly."

"Do you know where she is?"

"Yes, somewhere near Jax, Florida."

His voice now filled with rage. "Florida! Of course, she'd take her far away." He paused before he asked, "Who called you with this information? Do you know?"

"Yes, sir, Clive Jenkins."

"What? Are you sure?"

"Yes, sir I am." Jeff told him every word of Hank's and Clive's conversation, including his confession of murdering two men who were plotting to kidnap Megan.

There was a long pause from the judge. "Give me your number and a day or two to find out what can be done without you ending up in jail. You said Clive is going to call you back when he has a visual of her."

"Yes, sir."

"Okay, in the meantime, I'm going to find Florida case law on this subject. You call me the instant you hear from him. Let's hope he can keep her safe."

"I will and thank you."

The judge hung up.

"Hank.... what do we do?"

Hank's heart went out to Jeff, who by now was completely distraught, but without any idea on how to help him, he simply said, "We wait.... just like the judge said."

Jeff nodded as if he were defeated. "Can I have another drink? I need it."

Hank poured them both another shot and handed one to Jeff. In reality, it was only one swallow, but it seemed to appease him. Hank picked up the whiskey bottle and glasses then put everything back in the cupboard, just then Hope and Alice came in carrying lunch from their favorite Chinese restaurant.

* * *

Alice let out a loud squeal! "Hank.... Hank.... get the car, hurry! Baby's coming!"

Hope turned off the burners and put the food away while Jeff went to get the car. Hank ran to get the hospital bag that Alice put together so carefully and weight a ton.

They all piled in the car, men in front, Jeff in the driver's seat, the women were in back. The hospital was over two hours away and Hope was terrified that if there was a complication, Alice could lose her child. Every disaster that could happen in the next two hours ran through Hope's mind in a split second. *Stop it,* she admonished herself. *Nothing is going to happen.*

By the time they arrived at the hospital unscathed, Alice was in a great deal of pain. Hank leapt out of the car and burst through the emergency room doors. It seemed like only seconds before he emerged with an orderly and a gurney.

Hope felt utterly helpless in this situation. She knew nothing about giving birth or the amount of pain involved in childbirth. All she could do was hold her hand and wipe her face with a cold washcloth, something she had seen the midwives do when she was a teen. By the time they had Alice wheeled into the Emergency Room, Hope was a nervous wreck. She just sat in the car until she could get her emotions under control.

In the emergency room, the nurse was taking all of Alice's information. "How many children has she had?"

"None…."

"First time mom! Well, usually the first birth takes a while, in fact, it could take a day. Do you live close by?"

"No ma'am. We live in Flatbush, over two hours away."

She thought for a minute, "Mr. Hansen, your wife is going to need you with her. Mr. Olsen, you could get a motel room for resting and a hot shower. There is a nice one a block away with a restaurant attached. You can bring Mr. Hansen dinner if you like."

"Sounds good. Hank, Is that okay with you?"

"I would prefer it if you and Hope would go back home and run the store. We will be here for several days before Alice and the baby can go home. Isn't that, right?"

"Yes, that's true," said the nurse. "At least two days before the doctor would release them both."

Hank looked at Jeff. "Please…. people need to feed their animals."

The nurse said, "I'll see that he eats."

Jeff knew he was right. There was no need for all of us to be here. "Okay, if, you're sure."

"I'm sure. I promise to call you as soon as the baby's born…"

***

When they got home, Hope took one look at Jeff and knew instantly that something was wrong. "Jeff what's happened? Something happen to Alice or the baby?"

"No…they're fine. I didn't want to say anything with the new baby coming and all, Megan's in trouble…" **tug!** Jeff quickly looked around and when he didn't see anyone near him, he called out, "Garret are you here?" **Tug…!** Jeff nodded and continued; "Is it worse than we know?" **Tug!** Jeff nodded again. Does this have anything to do with her mother?" **Tug!** Jeff nodded. "Is she mistreating her?" **Tug!** Jeff nodded.

Hope, who had tears streaming down her face asked, "Can we help her?" Nothing… Jeff shook his head. Hope continued, "Is it that you don't know?" **Tug….!** Jeff nodded. "Okay, he doesn't know."

Jeff gaining more composure said, "We called Judge Haines and he's going to help us. But it will take a couple of days. Will you go and tell Megan that we are working on getting her out of there?" **Tug!** Jeff nodded. "Great thank you. Oh, and just so you know, Clive is nearby, and he is trying to help her too. So, keep a watchful eye out for him." **Tug, tug!** "Garrett, we need him to intervene if someone tries to kidnap her. There are already people plotting to do so. Until we can find a way to get her away from Irene legally, we need him to keep her safe. Understand?" **Tug...!** Jeff nodded. "Thank you. Now go and tell Megan we're coming to get her and that she needs to be brave for just a little while longer." **Tug!**

Jeff looked around, "I think he's gone. I don't feel him anymore."

"You could feel him?" Hope wanted to know.

"Yes....and...."

Hope held up both her hands and said, "Stop! Wait a minute. Clive and the judge! What happened while we were gone and start from the beginning."

Jeff filled in Hope, starting with the phone conversation with Clive which led them to call Judge Haines. "It's just that now we have to wait to see what the judge can find to help us legally."

Alice was pacing. "What has me stumped is Clive. What motive does he have for notifying us of Megan's condition? He could kidnap her for himself and simply disappear just like before?"

"Maybe he can't," said Jeff flatly. "He's a fugitive. I'm sure he has no means of support and is more than likely homeless. I'll bet he's barely surviving himself and to add Megan would probably be impossible."

"All good points, Jeff," Hope had to admit. "But are you insinuating that Clive has developed a heart?"

"I'm not saying that he has a heart," Jeff explained, "but I think the situation is so severe that even Clive finds her condition appalling. Hence the phone call and that though alone has me frightened. Clive did say that when he sees her, he will call us again."

"So, this is all hearsay?" asked Hope. "He actually hasn't seen her."

"What he told Hank was, the people who witnessed Megan's healing were commenting about how awful she looked."

Hope started crying. "Wait a minute. What aren't you telling me?"

Jeff shrugged. "Clive said that he overheard two men planning to kidnap her. So, he killed them."

The shock of hearing that statement stopped Hope cold in her tracks. "He is ruthless, which we already knew, but for him to say that outright is coldblooded."

"Maybe," agreed Jeff, "but he's the guy I want looking out for Megan right now."

* * *

Arriving two hours early, Clive drove around the marketplace twice. He had to make sure he had the perfect advantage point to watch her interact with others. That way he could analyze her condition better. Megan's booth was in the rear corner according to the sign which made it tricky to get a good place to observe her. *This woman is smarter than she looks*, he thought. *By taking the corner booth, Megan can't get out, she's trapped.*

There is a curtain across the front of the booth. Not sure what that's about, but a chair and a café table were off to the left. *Interesting*, he thought, *only one chair*.

The plaza was filling up with people looking to spend their money on trinkets and handmade goods. Musicians began plying lively music, *very festive*. Clive could feel his mood lightening up a bit and even found his foot unconsciously tapping to the rhythm. It was almost 9am and Clive held his breath as Irene came out from behind the curtain and sat down at the table. She had a medium-sized suitcase which she opened and set it on the floor beside her. At exactly 9am, she pulled out an 'Open' sign and hung it off the edge of the table.

She also placed a cash box in front of her. She pulled a cord and a sign unfurled which read, 'Megan the Magical Healer'.

Several people got in line and Irene called up the first customer. She took his money and told him to go behind the curtain!

No.... now what? He had no choice; he was going to have to go inside. He wasn't worried about Irene; they'd never met, but Megan might be a different story. As he stood in line, he repeatedly told himself that Megan wouldn't recognize him in disguise. *Oh geez, two to go!*

The closer he got he noticed that the curtain looked flimsy, not a heavy velvet so he couldn't talk freely. Oh crap, now what? The only thing he could think of was to write a note on the flyer and hand it to her. One to go! Clive's knees started to shake a bit, and sweat was beading up on his forehead. Crap! I'm next!

Unbeknownst to Clive, Irene was watching him and the crowd closely. When a tremor showed up in his hands, she relaxed concluding he definitely has medical problems. She had heard the murmurings of people wanting to take Meagan for themselves. When the guy came out, Irene turned to Clive and said, "Okay Sonny come on it's your turn?" Clive paid the one-hundred-dollar fee and went behind the curtain.

As he stepped inside the booth, Megan looked up and instantly recognized him. He quickly sat down and said, "Do you need this flyer back?" And shove the flyer towards her so she could see that there was writing on it. She shook her head, no, but read what was on the flyer. For a split second, her eyes lit up and then faded. She nodded and handed him back the flyer. Clive carefully put it back in his pocket and left, making sure to put on a show for Irene.

Now to find a phone and they aren't going to like what I found. He leaned against the corner of the building that led to the parking lot. Once he was satisfied that no one was surveilling the truck, he ran and jumped in. He hightailed it out of there to find a gas station where he could reverse the charges. It didn't take long to find an out-of-the-way gas station. He told the clerk that he wanted to use the phone and laid a $100 bill on the counter. The clerk talked to the operator and then handed the phone to Clive.

While he waited for someone to answer the phone, he actually felt horrible about what he had to tell them.

"Hank's feed...."

"It's Clive...." He paused.

Hank could tell by his somber tone; the news was not good. "It's bad, isn't it?"

"Worse actually, I'm sorry. Is Jeff around?"

"Yes, I'll get him."

Hank hollered for Jeff outside the back door. And he heard, "Coming!"

Jeff bolted through the loading dock door. "Is it Clive?" Hank only nodded and handed the phone to him. "Clive, I'm here. Tell me she's okay."

"Sorry, I can't say that. I couldn't just observe her because she was behind a curtain. So, I stood in line to see her. When I pulled the curtain back, I couldn't believe my eyes. But I didn't let on to her how shocked I was. You okay for me to continue?"

"Yes, I have to know."

"She is skin and bones, her hair is stringy like it hasn't been washed or brushed in a long while. Her knuckles have bruises and so do her arms. I'm pretty sure she was shackled to the floor."

"Did she recognize you?"

"Immediately, I think she was happy to see me."

"Yes, I can see where she would be. She was hoping you were going to kidnap her."

"Yes, I'm sure she was hoping for that, but when I passed her a note that said you were coming to get her, she smiled."

"Clive, we're waiting for the judge to tell us what we can do to get her out of there legally. Would you stick with her and then call us say tomorrow night. Oh, and do you know where they're headed to next?"

"Yes, two more nights here and then to Pensacola."

"Thank you and if you see anyone abusing her, please step in."

"Not a problem, I definitely will, I promise." Clive hung up.

The clerk gave him change from his phone call and the couple of apples he purchased.

Now to get back to the marketplace.

Chapter Sixteen
Leaving for Florida

Jeff returned the phone to the cradle and looked at Hank. "Never in my wildest dreams would I ever believe that I would be asking Clive to help me!"

"Me either, but what choice do you have?"

"None.... none at all."

The phone starts ringing and Hank answers, "Hank's Feed...."

"Judge Hines for Jeff Olsen...."

Hank hands the phone to Jeff. "Judge Hines...."

Jeff took the phone from Hank. "Hi judge...."

"Hi Jeff. Did you hear from Clive?"

"Yes. I just hung up from talking to him and judge, Clive says she's black and blue, starved but worse, Irene shackles her to the floor!"

The judge said flatly, "I need to see her, but how can we do that without kidnapping her?"

Hank smiled. "Arrest Irene for child abuse!"

"Can't," the judge retorted. "Unless someone files a complaint."

"That's easy, Judge what if we go and see her for ourselves and we find her in a horrible condition? We'll call the police!"

The judge said, "Do you have access to a camera?"

Hank's eyes lit up! "Just so happens I got a couple of digital ones yesterday. They are the new rage. I'll bet I can figure out how to use it pretty quickly."

"I've heard of them," said the judge. "Pictures would be the best documentation."

"Okay and if I get the pictures can we remove her immediately?"

"Yes…if you're serious about going to Florida, be very careful and don't let your emotions rule your actions and Jeff I'm talking to you."

"Yes sir, Hank will stop me before I do something stupid."

The judge hung up and Jeff chuckled, "So that means we're going to Florida!"

"Okay, the girls will be bringing lunch soon, we'll discuss it with them then."

"Perfect!"

* * *

Clive was almost giddy when he backed the truck into a parking space. He thought, I finally have a job protecting Megan from being kidnapped. If I'm successful, maybe one day I'll start a protection business for guarding famous people, politicians, diamond couriers, and CEOs of fortune five hundred companies! They all hire bodyguards. Now that I'm thinking about it, I'd be really good at this line of work.

Pulling out one of the apples and shining it on his shirt, the bite he took was so incredible that he nearly missed seeing the squad car parked near the front entrance. Oh damn! He scrambled to get all his stuff into his backpack and got out of the stolen truck as fast as he could. He turned around and looked for a place to hide. A corner or a crevice between two buildings would be ideal, he thought. He looked everywhere searching for the perfect place and spotted Irene's truck parked behind her booth. I could hide in the back! *Why not?* He thought *it was perfect! It's a stake bed truck, and if I'm not mistaken, it looks like there are several crates in the back.* He peeked inside, *I could hide underneath one of those tarps, I doubt if she uses all of them. I just hope the police leave soon.* He looked at the watch he took off one of the dead guys, there were three hours left before Irene would close up shop. *I need to use the outhouse and eat.*

He was about to head over to the outhouse when he heard, "John, keep an eye on that truck. He's here and we're going to find him. He's not going to escape this time."

Clive grabbed a tarp and put it over him and laid as still as he possibly could. There was movement all around him, people running around the parking lot, and he dared not look through the slates. The space between the slats was at least four or more inches high, they could easily see him looking out.

That same voice was issuing orders again, "You two block off the front entrance and get James and Cliff to take the back exit. Check those cars thoroughly, even in the trunk and you other two, check every booth inside." The men responded with, "Yes sir."

A different voice asked, "What about bringing in a K-9 unit?"

"No, too many people tramping through here. The scent is already compromised, but they can patrol the perimeter, in case he tries to run. Oh man, I hope he runs. I have a bullet with his name on it!"

Clive thought, that sounds like a threat, remind me to look you up later officer…where is he? He sounds like he's right up against this truck!

"Hey Sarge, the parking lot has been cleared, except this truck."

"There are two crates, one with children's clothing female and the other held women's clothing. There are several tarps, no doubt to cover their supplies once she closes down her booth. The sign on her booth says she's going to be here one more night."

"Okay then…., the booths are clear too. He's not here."

"That's a shame," he paused. "Double check every face that leaves here. We'll be here an hour before they open in the morning. Oh, and disable that truck. I don't want to leave a guard here overnight."

"Yes sir."

Within thirty minutes, all the police had moved to the exits. Clive could finally breath and move around. Every muscle and bone in his body ached from lying flat for the past three hours. He rushed to get out of the truck before his bladder burst. Relief finally, now to find food and he better hurry, the marketplace was closing down in about ten minutes. He knew there was a Mexican stand two booths away, because he'd smelled the spicy aroma all afternoon.

I still have to be careful, so I'm not recognized by the feds or the police. I need a disguise of some sort.

His stomach growled so loud; he was sure the whole county heard it. *Okay, okay, simmer down, I'm working on it!*

He leaned against the back of someone's booth near the truck, just gazing across the near empty parking lot. He spotted a tool belt lying in the dirt. Someone left it on the bumper or tailgate and when they left it fell off. How fortuitous for him and immediately strolled over to pick it up. He quickly put it on and although a bit large, he managed to get it to stay up.

Pulling out some cash, he went to the Mexican food booth and ordered three burritos. He made sure his back was to the exits. Waiting for his food to cook gave him the perfect advantage to access Megan's booth. There were still three customers in line. He needed to eat and get back in the truck as quickly as he could. Finally, his food arrived, and he thanked the lady. He picked up the burritos and headed back. Climbing under the tarp, he ate.

It wasn't ten minutes before he felt someone climb into the flatbed. Furniture was being placed on top of him. was not sure who was loading the truck, so he decided to wait until everything was loaded before he peeked. But he didn't have to peek, the ankle chain was dragging on the floor. He was about to make himself known when he heard a sarcastic voice say, "Stack that right...."

"I will once it's all in here!"

"Watch your mouth, little witch or I'll withhold your dinner again. You'll be really hungry by morning...."

No response from Megan, she just kept moving furniture around the truck.

"You're not talking now, smart mouth?"

The movement continued.

"No dinner for you!" She stalked off to get in the cab of the truck and slammed the door.

"Clive, I know you're here, but stay hidden until she pulls out of here."

"Okay, there's a burrito under your dress in the crate, oh, and an apple."

"Thank you," she whispered.

"Fifteen minutes later, Megan knocked on the window of the cab. Irene came out and walked to the back of the truck.

"Looks good. Still no dinner. Get in position." Megan did and Irene chained her to the slat and the metal post. "Grab the tarp and cover yourself,"

The canvas rustled, the truck started up and she headed for the exit.

Clive asked, "Megan are you shackled?"

"Yes.... now quiet. We'll talk in a few minutes."

The truck slowed, no doubt to exit the gate. Words were spoken with the guard, but Clive couldn't hear what was said. Once she passed the gate, Irene took off like a bat out of hell. The truck sounded like it was falling apart.

"Damn," said Clive. "Does she drive like this all the time?"

"No, all those cops made her really nervous, I'm sure we are headed to the next town."

"What happens when we get to the next city?"

"She'll get a room…."

"Where do you sleep?"

"Here in the truck."

Clive had to think about that for a minute. A plan was forming in his mind, but there was one thing he needed the answer to, "Megan, why are you shackled?"

"I tried to run away a bunch of times."

Of course, you did! "You eat, I'm going to think a minute. Okay?"

"Sure…."

Clive could hear her rummaging through the crate to find the burrito and the apple. From the sounds she was making, she hadn't eaten in a while.

"Megan, slow down. You're going to make yourself sick."

"Okay…."

"Good girl…."

He waited until she stopped eating before he asked, "What does she do when she goes to check into the hotel?"

"Well, she goes inside and gets the room key, and then she comes out here to give me my pillow and tells me to be quiet all night."

"Okay thank you. I'm going to think for a little while, and while I do, you rest."

"Yes, I will. I'm very tired."

They were so many questions that he wanted to ask her. But all that would have to wait until he got her away from Irene and they were safe. His plan will work easily, so he used his backpack for a pillow and fell sound asleep.

Chapter Seventeen
Florida

Hank and Jeff retrieved their luggage off the turnstile and headed to the car rental booth. The judge had set them up with the car, but they had no idea it would be a van. After signing all the paperwork, they climbed into the van only to find out that it was a camper van! It had a small kitchen, cupboards, a toilet and two bunkbeds. Perfect for what they needed. *Thank you Judge!*

"Food first," said Hank. "I'm starved."

"Me too! Any suggestions?"

"Yes, see that diner across the street?"

"Yes, the one that says, all night?"

"That's the one!"

Hank slid in behind the wheel and cranked the motor. "Purrs like a kitten…"

"Probably slower than dirt."

Hank goosed the gas pedal, and it jumped off the ground! "Holy crap lots of power too!"

Jeff laughed, "who knew?"

Parking the van far away from other vehicles, they climbed out and headed for the front door. Jeff was surprised at how many customers were inside. *Must be traffic from the airport. People are always hungry when traveling.*

The waitress seated them and went to get their coffee's. By the time she returned, they had decided on what they wanted to eat.

They both ordered steak and eggs with fried potatoes and sourdough toast.

Jeff whispered, "We need to call Alice and see if Clive called."

"Eat first," said Hank sternly.

"Okay...." *Touchy, isn't he?*

It's a good thing the food arrived when it did, as Hank was about to eat the table. *I don't think I have ever seen a human being so hungry!*

It wasn't until he had eaten half his meal, did Hank take a breath and started to relax.

"Are you alright?"

"Yes...."

Okay, still not ready to be civil.

Finally, the meal was over, the waitress took away the plates and she was bringing more coffee. When she returned, Hank asked where he could find a pay telephone.

"Hanging on the wall." She pointed toward the restroom.

"Thanks," he said politely and got up to make the call.

Megan's here somewhere and we just have to find her. **Tug**. *Garrett, can you hear my thoughts?* **Tug**. *That's awesome! We need you to stay with us now that we're in Florida. It would be easy for us to get into trouble or get turned around somehow. Will you stay with us please?* **Tug**.... *Thank you. Hey, wait a minute, Garrett if you can hear my thoughts, can I hear your thoughts?* **Tug, tug, tug**. *Does that mean you don't know.* **Tug**. *Well then try talking to me and let's see what happens.*

Can you hear me, Jeff?

I can hear you!

Hank returned and had a lot of information. Alice said Clive called in the middle of the night and left a message that said, not in

Jax Florida on the way to Fort Myer. I fed Megan probably the first good meal she's had in a long while. I don't know where in Fort Myers we will be but look for a black stake bed truck with two crates and a bunch of tarps in the back, I'm hiding under the tarps. Pennsylvania license plates, 43HYP56. I will try to call tomorrow to let you know exactly where we are.

Alice told him that we were in Florida.

"That's awesome! I have news too."

"You do?"

"Yes, I do. While you were making your call, I was thinking that Megan was here somewhere and that we needed to find her. I got a tug on my shirt. So, I asked Garrett if he could hear my thoughts and with the tugs, he said he could. Again, I asked Garrett, if you can hear my thoughts, then can I hear yours. He said he didn't know. I asked him to try and lo and behold I heard him!"

"Is he here now?"

"Yes.... and I asked him to stay with us until we find Megan."

Hank chuckled, "I hope he doesn't snore!"

Garrett reached over and punched Hank's shoulder.

Hank's eyes widened, "Hey, I felt that!"

***

After making his phone call to Alice, Clive snuck back into the truck bed and just in the nick of time too. Irene came and took Megan away, he hoped she would feed her dinner and give her a bath, which gave him time to think about Alice's message. She told him that the judge wanted pictures of Megan's condition. That would require a camera. I wonder if they sell those in the motel's office. I didn't pay attention while I was there.

Clive left the truck and headed for the office just as Irene was bringing Megan back. Hopefully, he was far enough away that she didn't see where he was coming from. As luck would have it there were several cars parked not far from her truck. Surely, she would think I came from one of those vehicles and not hers.

He went into the office and asked, "Do you have cameras?"

"Yes, disposables. They are just as good as a regular camera, but when you are finished with the roll, you develop them and throw the camera away. People on vacation love them!"

"Sounds perfect! I'll take one."

"Certainly, sir. Twenty-four dollars...."

As Clive paid the clerk, he asked, "is there a grocery store nearby?"

"Yes, a small one! Around the corner and down about a half a block, it's called Speedy Mart."

"Thanks...." He left the office and headed toward the grocery store. The hairs on his neck bristled, he was positive Irene was watching him and hopefully, by the time he returned she would be back in her room. *There's no way to know if she's back in her room, so I'll put my plan into action tonight.*

The grocery store was packed with vacationers. The shelves were almost empty this late in the day, but he managed to find two bananas and two ready-made sandwiches.

As he was walking back to the hotel, a revelation hit him. *I'll rent a room of my own and I'll get her out of that truck and put her in the room with me. That way when Irene comes out and find her gone, she won't know where to look and assume that she ran away again.* That's actually better than the plan he had before.

When he came around the end of the motel, he looked at the parking lot and Irene's truck was leaving the parking lot. In the place where the truck had been parked was his backpack. He ran over there and picked it up and quickly opened it. Inside was a note from Megan, that said they were going on to Fort Myer tonight. Damn I screwed up again. What to do, what to do…?

After thinking about his newfound situation, he decided to get a room. He went back into the office purchased a room for the night, and once inside, he sat down on the bed. He only had one option, to call Alice, and tell her where he was exactly. That way, Hank and Jeff could find him. He hated to tell Alice that he'd lost Megan, but he had no choice. Picking up the phone, he made the call. *Now I wait.*

Alice paced as she watched the clock. Hank was supposed to call in thirty minutes, and it seemed like an eternity. Hope is going to be devastated that Clive lost Megan again.

Hank and Jeff decided on a restaurant called Cracker Barrel for dinner. Once they were seated and gave their order to the waiter, Hank went to call Alice.

Finally, the phone rang, and Alice picked it up, "Hello Hank!"

"Yes honey, it's me any news from Clive?"

"Yes, he's off route seventy-five, in Solana, Florida, hotel is the Ramada Inn room, 202. It's the only hotel in town. And Hank he lost Megan again."

"How?"

"He went to get her food, and when he came back, they were driving out the driveway. Megan did manage to leave him his backpack, and in and it was a note that said they were going onto Fort Myers."

"Okay, we'll catch up with him there."

"Be careful please."

"We will, I promise. I'll call you about this same time tomorrow."

"Okay, bye."

Hank returned to the table and told Jeff what Alice had told him.

Jeff was silent for a bit. "Did you bring in the map?"

"Yes, I did." Hey, reached into his back pocket and pulled out the map. He spread the map across the table. "According to Alice, he's held up in a Ramada Inn in Solana, Florida, here!"

"We're not far, maybe an hour."

Hank refolded the map and put it back in his pocket. Their dinners arrive shortly thereafter but neither of them felt like eating.

Jeff looked at his perfectly cooked T-bone steak and put down his fork. "Maybe, I'll eat this later. I can't right now."

"Sounds good to me too." Hank signaled for the waiter to come over. "Can we get these dinners to go?"

"Certainly, sir." He picked up their plates and whisked them away. Two minutes later, he returned with their food packaged and the check.

The two dinners took up the whole interior of the tiny fridge. At least they'll be easy to reheat when we feel like eating, thought Jeff as he climbed into the passenger seat.

"I really have mixed feelings about this meeting with Clive," confessed Jeff.

"Yes, I know the feeling, let's get it over with."

Jeff nodded as Hank pulled out of the parking lot. It seemed like it only took seconds to get to the hotel but in actuality, it was 40 minutes. Jeff hopped out and went into the lobby to find a house phone. He picked it up and dial 202.

Clive answered, "hello…."

"It's Jeff, we're in the lobby."

"Come on up."

The room is easy to find. Hank and Jeff looked at each other before they knocked.

Clive opened the door and stood aside to allow them to enter. Hank and Jeff sat at the settee table while Clive sat on the bed.

Clive immediately said, "I didn't find out about having a camera until it was too late. But I did draw everything for you." He handed a tablet to Jeff.

The drawings were impressive and graphic. They portrayed the torture that Megan had to endure. Jeff started to tear it up while Hank, on the other hand, had to look away. One picture depicted Megan shackled to the floor while she worked. The next, shackled again to the side of the truck, and the last one was of Irene dragging her around by the hair.

Jeff looked over at Clive. "These drawings are impressive."

"Thanks. I had some time on my hands," he paused. "I'm angry because I was five minutes away from getting her out of Irene's clutches. I had bought the camera, and I was coming around the corner, only to watch them drive away."

"What do you think happened?" Hank asked.

"I think what started it was when we were in Jax. Someone recognized me and called the police. The whole place was surrounded, of course they didn't find me, but I think she is a bit paranoid. She has to know that putting shackles on a person is wrong. So, at the end of the day, Megan packed up the truck and as soon as Irene left that parking lot, she stepped into high gear. She told Megan that they would not be returning for the last day, and they were going onto Fort Mayers."

Hank leaned in, "so that's how you ended up here?"

"Yes. I didn't know if she was going to feed her so while she had Megan upstairs in her room, I went to the store for a couple sandwiches and bananas. I was on my way back when I saw them pulling out of the driveway. I really don't know why she ran this time."

"Okay let's get going," said Hank. "You can't be safe here either."

"Probably not…." Clive picked up his backpack and they all walked out the door.

Once they got Clive settled in the van, Hank got the map out from the visor. "Fort Mayers….it appears that it too is only an hour away."

Tug. Garrett, do you know where Megan is exactly?

Yes.

Will you direct us?

Yes!

Thank you….

"Garrett just told me that he knows exactly where Megan is, and he is going to direct us."

Clive turned pale, "Garrett! Seriously?"

"Yes Clive…. "Garrett," replied Jeff. "Something wrong…?"

"Not unless he's going to tear up your van like he did my office….!"

"Not our van. The judge rented it for us."

"The same judge who gave her back to her mother, that judge?"

Jeff was getting irritated with Clive's sarcastic remarks, no matter how accurate they are, "Yes, that judge. He tried everything he could think of to *not* give her to Irene, everything! Family court overruled his every objection."

Get off next exit….

Okay Garrett

"Get off next exit…."

"Okay….," said Hank. "We must be close. Get the cameras ready. We may not have a whole lot of time to get her free."

Turn left at the signal.

Hank, turn left…

Clive pointed to a truck in the parking lot of a rundown motel. "That's her truck!"

"Garrett, we need you to go to see if Megan is alone. Understood?"

"Yes"

They waited poised for action. Surely, Irene will be asleep, it's almost midnight.

Jeff heard, *alone!*

"She's alone, get the cameras ready," said Hank.

With cameras in hand, and Hank's bolt cutters, they approach the truck. Hank pulled back the tarp. He was horrified by her condition, and he used the bolt cutters to cut the chain on the shackles. "Get her in the van hurry."

Jeff picked her up while Clive opened the van door. Hank jumped off the truck bed as a shot rang out hitting him in the shoulder.

Irene hollered out, "next one will be in your brain."

"Get in both of you," ordered Clive. "I'll take care of Irene."

"Cops will be here in a few minutes," Jeff warned.

"Get going…now!"

Another shot rang out, this one hit the van. With everybody on board, Jeff took off. First priority, find a hospital for Hank and Megan. She crawled over to Hank.

"No Megan don't heal him, I need the police to see him and you., understand?"

"Yes, I think so, but there is so much blood!"

"She must have hit an artery. Can you stop the bleeding without healing him?"

"Yes."

"Okay do it…. hey, Megan, how are you?"

"I'll be okay now that you're here."

"We have missed you terribly."

Megan got up off the floor and climbed up on the sofa so she could wrap her arms around Jeff's neck. He patted her arms affectionately.

"How's Hank doing?"

"I don't know, he's asleep." Megan looked over at Hank. He started to convulse. "Oh no!" Cried out Megan and jumped down to kneel down beside him.

"What's happening Megan?"

"He's jumping all over the floor!"

"Crap….!"

Finally, he saw a sign that said Hospital with an arrow pointing straight ahead, so he floored it. As he pulled into the Emergency parking, he started yelling, "I need help!"

Two paramedics, who were about to leave, ran to the van. Jeff said to Garrett, "stay with Megan. Do not leave her side, understood?"

Tug!

The van door opened. Jeff pointed to Hank, "gunshot…he's really bad. We were rescuing Megan and he was shot."

One paramedic ran to get a doctor and get gurneys. The paramedic noticed Megan and her shackles, "are you serious? This girl was shackled to something?"

"Yes! A stake-bed truck!" Jeff jumped out and ran around to the other side as the first gurney and two attendants arrived. They loaded Hank onto the gurney and took off toward the doors. The paramedic that remained lifted Megan in his arms and he too, ran for the doors. To Jeff he said, "come with me."

Jeff closed the van door and fell in step with him. Once inside, he looked for Hank and found him surrounded by doctors and nurses, all of them issuing orders. But all Jeff heard was the machine's high-pitched squeal, Hank had flatlined.

"Megan! Hank died!"

Megan wiggled out of the paramedic's arms and ran for Hank. They all tried to stop us from reaching him. Jeff screamed, "let us through; she can save him!"

The bewildered medical staff backed away. Megan grabbed Hank's hand and with her left, she put it on his chest. Her index finger started tapping his chest, she buried her face in his shoulder and began her chanting. Jeff could see the skepticism on their faces, but he didn't care.

It took longer than Jeff thought it should, but the cardiac machine suddenly beeped showing one heartbeat, then another and finally sinus-rhythm. The doctor started to head toward Hank, but Jeff held him back. "She's not done." To Megan he said, "can you get the bullet out? The police will need it." Megan nodded.

With her left hand, she started drawing circles around the wound and the bullet eased up to the surface.

"Thank you," Jeff smiled at Megan. "Now heal him completely, please." Megan nodded.

Within minutes, Hank opened his eyes and sat up! He spotted Megan and held out his arms to which she climbed into. You could hear a pin drop in the ER room.

Jeff hadn't noticed that the police had arrived and were videotaping the whole thing. An officer stepped forward and whispered, "I'll take that bullet. And sir if you will come with me."

"I will gladly go with you, but not until she is photographed, and those shackles removed."

"We can do that at the police station, sir."

Jeff looked at Hank, "Ae you okay for now?"

"Yes…"

The doctor said, "We'd like to check him over to make sure."

"Yes, of course," Jeff rolled his eyes so only Hank could see. "We'll be back as soon as we can. The police want to talk to us."

"Go, I'll be fine."

Jeff took Megan from Hank and carried her out of the ER. A nurse came out of nowhere and handed Jeff two bottles of water. "See that she drinks these, both of them."

"Yes, ma'am and thank you."

The officer opened the back door for Jeff. He slid in still holding tightly to Megan. She weighed nothing in his arms, and he wouldn't let his mind wander to why she was so light. He knew why, he just couldn't believe that Irene would do this to her.

The police station was literally in the next block. The officer hit a button on his steering wheel and a gate swung open and the officer drove down inside the building.

Wow…. thought Jeff. We're going down into a basement!

At the bottom of the ramp, he stopped and got out to open Jeff's door. He slid Megan off his lap long enough to get out himself, and then picked her up.

"Follow me, sir." Jeff nodded.

The room he took them to was of a medium-size cement cavern. There was a small table with four chairs. The door opened and a woman came in holding a large camera.

"Is she awake?" Asked the woman.

"Yes, she's just terrified," explained Jeff. "I'll help her."

Jeff went to set her down on the tabletop and Megan wouldn't let go. "Megan, this lady is going to take pictures for, Judge Hines, okay?" Megan nodded. "And, then we can take off these horrid shackles. I'll hold your hand, okay?"

Megan nodded and sat up straight. She followed every direction the photographer gave her.

Softly the woman whispered to Jeff, "I need to see her back." Megan began to cry but lifted the dress over her head.

Jeff sucked in his breath and whispered, "Oh Megan! I am *so* sorry." He, too, began to cry at the sight of the scarring from many beatings with a belt or strap of some kind.

"The buttocks?"

Megan quickly looked at Jeff, he nodded, "Megan, let's get this over with, okay?" She nodded and pulled down her filthy underwear.

Now the photographer was tearing up. The officer asked, "What did she hit you with?"

"A strap…. I think. I'm not sure though."

"Okay baby, let me take those shackles off." The officer came toward her holding a screwdriver. Megan held out each hand, one at a time. Next, we're her ankles. The shackles were put into an evidence bag. A female officer came in and explained that they needed her clothing.

She said, "I hope you like orange! I cut a man's shirt down, so your body is covered, I wish I had a pretty dress for you to wear."

Jeff whispered, "She'll have a dress as soon as we get her cleaned up."

The original officer, who brought them to the station, turned and faced the wall.

"Okay, let's get these rags off of you!"

Megan turned to face the officer and put her hands up in the air. The officer lifted the dress off and shuddered. Jeff caught her look of disgust.

Into a mini microphone that was pinned to her shirt, she said, "Sarah…come back in here and bring your camera."

Jeff terrified asked, "What is it?"

"Don't look…." Her eyes were pleading with him not to look. He nodded. "Where did these come from?"

"When I was bad, she cut those to let the devil out."

"Do they hurt?"

"Not really. I can take the pain away."

Jeff nodded to validate that she could.

The photographer entered the room and stopped in mid-stride. She took a few seconds to compose herself and only then did she take the photographs. The pain in her eyes was palpable and when she taken the required photographs, she ran out of the room.

As the officer removed the dress completely, she said, "Okay, Megan we are finished with the photographs and lift your arms again, I'm going to put the big shirt on you. Hey, can you tell me how you take the pain away?"

"I don't know how I do it, I just know I can." Megan looked up at the officer, "I see that you have a sore foot."

"Yes, I do. Why?"

"I will fix it for you, if you want me to!"

"You can fix it completely?" She nodded. The officer looked at Jeff and he nodded. "Okay go for it." She sat down in the chair and put the injured foot forward.

Megan sat down on the floor in front of the officer and wrapped her tiny hands around the bandaged ankle. Megan began her chant. After a few minutes, Megan let go and stood up. "Okay ma'am, you can stand up now."

"You sure I won't fall down and break my butt!"

Megan giggled. "It's fixed now, you won't fall, I promise!"

The officer stood up and put her hands on her butt just in case she fell on the floor. Megan giggled like crazy! The ankle that had given her so much pain for three days did not hurt at all. She sat down and lifted her pant leg to take off the bandage. Prior, the ankle was so swollen, not to mention black and blue. However, after she unwrapped it, it was like nothing ever happened. She looked over at Jeff and asked, "This is why she was shackled, isn't it? The mother was afraid someone would take her."

Jeff nodded. However, it was Megan who gave them the final clue into Irene's delusions, "She could hear people's thoughts and they wanted to take me away so I could make money for them!"

"Hence the paranoia…" murmured the officer.

"I don't know what that means," Megan confessed, "but she seemed afraid all the time."

The officer hugged Megan tightly. "You are an extraordinary little girl. I want to thank you for fixing my ankle and for being so good through all of our poking and prodding. Not many children, your age would sit still and be so good."

"You're welcome, ma'am. I'm just happy that Jeff found me."

"You are still going to have to go back to the hospital and be checked out by a doctor and then you can go home. Is that okay with you?"

"Yes ma'am, it is."

"Chuck, will you take them back to the hospital please? I'll join you in a minute."

"Yes, I'll be happy to."

They no sooner walked into the ER when a nurse came over to greet Jeff and Megan, she said, "I'll take her from here."

Jeff told Megan, "I'll be right here when you get back, I promise."

"Okay…"

Within seconds, she was gone behind the curtain, Jeff came apart. Hank was coming in from overseeing the investigation of the van. He took one look at Jeff, and he ran to catch him as he collapsed. Finding the closest bench, Hank lowered him onto it.

"Jeff what happened?"

"Irene cut her, starved her and beat her. If I ever get my hands on that woman, they will have to kill me to get me off of her." Jeff was shaking with rage, so badly that Hank stopped an orderly and requested a doctor to come and look at him.

The orderly took one look at Jeff and said, "Right away, sir."

Jeff was still shaking when the doctor appeared a few minutes later. "What's the matter?"

"We rescued his daughter from a cold-blooded killer and her psychopathic mother. I think this is an adrenaline release. He can't stop shaking."

"Good call…I'll be right back."

The doctor reappeared and gave him a shot, "Keep an eye on him. I'm going to have an orderly bring a gurney. He'll be safer on one."

"Yes sir."

Chapter Eighteen
The Takedown

Clive ducked behind the building and maneuvered himself as close to the truck as possible. The instant Irene ran back to her room, no doubt to pack, he got into the back of the truck. The police would be here any minute, surely someone called them with a 'shots fired' code. He also thought she would get on the freeway and get as far away as possible, but she didn't. She only went a few blocks to another hotel, parked in the back, and went in to get a room.

How odd! What is she doing? The instant she was out of sight, he got out of the truck and walked across the street to an all-night restaurant. Taking a booth that had a window facing the hotel, he ordered a cup of coffee. Although he was starving, he told her to hold off putting in his order until he had drank the cup of coffee. He needed to unwind a bit before he could actually eat.

Clive knew what he had to do, call the police, and tell them where she was. Eat first, then call, he decided. That call would mean that he would be on the street again. The money in his pocket will not last forever. Although Fort Mayer was big enough that he could survive, he was tired of scrounging for food and shelter.

The waitress came by to refill his cup, he looked up at her and nodded.

"Okay sir, it will be up in a jiffy."

"Thank you..."

The steak was cooked to perfection and if the truth was known, he could have eaten another one. But that meant becoming overstuffed, gassy, and miserable. The one thing he'd learned from his time on the run was restraint, do not overeat because bathrooms were hard to find, especially in the middle of the night.

He decided that he had stalled long enough. It was time to make the call. Laying two twenties on the table, he headed for the phone booth.

Dialing 911 he waited for someone to answer, finally he heard, "911 what's your emergency?"

"I have information as to the whereabouts of Irene Cob?"

"Where is she?"

"In the Best Western on highway 92, bottom floor. I can't see the room number from here.

He walked over to the little grocery across from the hotel. He had to find another disguise. Quickly scouring the shelves, he came across black shoe polish and paused for a split second. *Perfect*, he thought and purchased the polish. Running behind the store, he opened the tin, and immediately began rubbing the black goo all over his exposed body parts. *Don't forget ears, back of the neck, and ankles,* he told himself. As soon as he felt he was completely covered, he went back and sat down on the bench in front of the grocery. The first siren could be heard approaching in the distance. *This is going to be good,* he thought. Smiling like a Cheshire cat, he anticipated when the sirens would cut off as they definitely didn't want her to notice them arriving. The sirens turned off; they must be closed now.

The first squad car rolled into the parking lot in stealth mode, two then three cars joined. Others went around back, making sure she couldn't escape.

Clive held his breath as three officers approached her door. One officer tapped on the door with his billy-club. No answer!

Clive chuckled as he thought. Did you think she'd open the door and invite you in for coffee? Geez guys, of course, she's not going to answer!

They called out her name a few more times, no response. Another officer used a master key to open the door. Carefully, with his foot, he pushed open the door and jumped back. Blam…blam…the shots rang out.

Oh crap! She's shooting at the officers! They're going to go in guns blazing! Clive tried not to watch but he couldn't take his eyes off Irene's door.

An officer tried to peek into her room but was met with gunfire and her yelling for him to go away!

Oh! That ain't going to happen Irene!

Officers were evacuating the rooms on either side of her's and the one below. Once they accomplished those tasks, they focused on Irene and her capture. Every time an officer started talking to her she'd shoot.

Sooner or later, she'll run out of bullets, and they'd have to go in and then what? They might end up killing her or if they are able to capture her, a state hospital for the criminally insane is in her future! Clive wasn't sure what he hoped would happen to her, but Irene was a mentally ill woman. She was completely off her rocker, but should she die? Yes, he thought, most certainly.

It looks like they've quit talking to her. Clive was poised, like a lion ready to spring on a tasty morsel. Do something, anything, just get it over with! The anticipation is killing me. Ut oh! Gas masks! They are going to smoke her out!

A helicopter was circling overhead. Where did that come from? He laughed, *news at eleven!*

Here we go! They tossed a smoke bomb into her room and stood back. Smoke billowed out the door, but no Irene! *Interesting, surely, she has to be choking by now.* An officer peeked inside the door, Blam! The officer fell to the floor. Two officers started shooting into the room and then stopped. They entered the room to find Irene dead!

Clive breathed a sigh of relief. He got up and went into the store to make a call to Alice and Hope.

Alice answered the phone, "Hank's Feed and Grain."

"It's Clive…Irene is dead." He hung up and left the grocery. The coroner arrived to remove Irene's body. The downed officer must have been taken to the hospital already, he was no longer laying in the doorway.

Clive just sat on the bench, watching the police work the scene. It was over, Irene was dead and hopefully Megan could live a normal life. Whatever that looks like for her.

Too bad Irene's room will go to waste. A soft bed sounds incredibly good right now and decided that he would rent a room for one more night.

Chapter Nineteen
Recovery

Jeff looks so peaceful laying on the gurney. The shot the doctor gave him must have been a whopper, thought Hank. Jeff is a tough guy usually. What he saw on Megan's body was more than he could bear and from the description, Jeff wasn't the only one who broke down. I'm so glad I wasn't in that room; I don't know what I would have done. Maybe I'd be in a looney-bin myself.

An orderly came into the cubicle and raised the guard rails on both sides. "Don't want him to wake up confused and try to stand up. Won't be pretty when he hits the floor."

"Thanks…"

"You're welcome."

"I'd like to make a phone call. Will he be okay for a few minutes?"

"Yes, at least for another hour or so. Is that enough time?"

"Plenty.…"

"Go make your call, I'll keep an eye on him."

"Thank you and his wife will thank you too." Hank got up and went to the lobby where there were phone booths. He paused, then said to no one. "I don't want to make this call."

The phone rang on the other end and Hank prayed that he could get through it.

"Hank's Feed and Grain!"

"Hi Alice.…"

"Hey honey, how are you holding up?"

"I'm doing okay, it's Jeff that needs the help."

"What happened?"

Hank told her what he knew about Megan's abuse and about Jeff's condition. I'm sure he will be fine, but right now he's an emotional mess."

"Megan?"

"She's still in with the doctors. So, I don't know much."

Alice hesitated before she said, "I need to tell you that Clive called about thirty minutes ago, Irene is dead."

"Good…when the whole story comes out about her…." Hank's voice faltered.

"Hank it's alright. Her death is all over the news and Clive had nothing to do with it other than telling the police her location."

"Good…I was worried that he might have killed her himself."

"No, not this time. When will you be coming home?"

"Next day or two. I'll let you know."

"Okay, I love you, be safe."

"Love you, too." Hank hung up and went to the coffee machine for a cup of crappy instant hospital coffee, but it will have to do. He sat back down in the chair beside Jeff. Poor guy was still out cold.

On the wall across the hall was a TV and the news was on. He got up and went out where he could hear the newscaster describing Irene's takedown and Megan's injuries. He even had trouble getting through all the horrific atrocities that Irene put her through. The newscaster looked extremely pleased to announce that Irene had been killed in a standoff with the police.

Clive, you deserve a medal, if only you hadn't killed all those other people.

Jeff was waking up and Megan was being brought out. The photographer, Sarah, came through the doors with bags of clothes for Megan.

Sarah took her behind a curtain where a lot of giggling ensued. "What happened to your cuts?"

"I showed the doctor how I could heal them."

"You are an extraordinary little girl. Let's show your dad how beautiful you are."

In a few minutes, Megan popped out from behind the curtain, "Look Jeff!"

"Oh Megan, you are so beautiful in that blue dress! Thank you, Sarah. Let me pay you…."

She cut him off, "This was my honor and pleasure."

Jeff nodded. Doctor Jenkins came around the corner. "You can take her home as soon as I give you instructions. Come with me. And Miss Hollis it was an honor to meet you."

"Thank you."

Jeff followed the doctor into his office. "Please have a seat."

Okay, thought Jeff. Something is wrong.

"I have the results of her bloodwork and X-rays. And I must say, I'm baffled." He paused. "I could write journals about these x-rays and still might, without names, of course. I wish I understood what I'm looking at, but I don't."

Jeff sat forward, "What are you talking about?"

"Well, she presents with regenerative blood cells, which simply means self-healing."

Puzzled by the term self-healing, Jeff asked, "Is that bad?"

"No, not really."

"Okay, so what are you saying?"

"She looks human, but I'm positive she isn't …."

Jeff was actually not surprised, "So what is she?"

"Immortal."

"That explains everything!" Jeff looked at the doctor. "What are you going to do with this information?"

"If I say anything at all, she'll be put in a science lab for study. And, with all she's been through, I really don't want to do that."

"So, what then?"

The doctor eyed Jeff carefully. "I'd like to make a deal with you."

"What kind of deal?"

"For my silence, would you bring her here every five years for testing?"

Jeff was stunned and sat back in his seat and thought, *this doctor is bribing me!* "It's a cheap price for your silence, why so cheap?"

"If I had my way, I'd shout this from the rooftops! But I will take a monitoring position if you'll let me. I'd like to see how she evolves into adulthood."

Jeff had to take a minute and think about what this would mean for Megan. There is a definite plus for her with not having to explain her uniqueness every time she needs to see a doctor. "Yes, I will. In fact, now that I think about it, that will be perfect. She needs a doctor that understands her."

"Thank you. But if she ever needs a doctor, which I doubt, you call me immediately, agreed?" Jeff nodded. "If you have any questions ask them now. If not, let's join the others."

Jeff stood up and followed the doctor back to the ER.

After an exchange of a few pleasantries, the doctor and Sarah left. Jeff, Megan, and Hank walked out of the hospital and climbed into their bullet riddled van.

Hank whispered, "Let's get out of here and go home."

Jeff put his hand on Hank's arm. "Just a minute, I need to talk to Garrett about something. I'll fill you in, in a couple of minutes, okay?"

"Sure...."

Garrett, I need to talk to you!

I'm here.

Did you know that she's an alien?

No, but we suspected. I remember hearing claims that Irene was presumed crazy when she screamed all around the village that a spaceship came an abducted her, although no one said they believed her. She gave birth to Megan in the sanitarium.

Do you know what country she was born in?

Yes, we adopted her in Romania when she was a newborn.

That helps a lot. Thank you! And Garrett, we will protect her.

I know and thank you.

"Okay, Hank let's hit the road."

All the way to the airport, Jeff was perplexed about who needed to know about Megan's origin. He decided that no one else needs to know besides me and the doctor. His concern was that they could become leery or even frightful of her as she got older. Who knows the full extent of her powers!

Megan heard every word of Jeff and her dad's conversation and thought, I am an alien, that does feel right to me. At least I'm not alone as there are others. I hear them talking in the background. Maybe one day, I will find them, or they will find me.

***

A week later, they all stood before Judge Haines, including Hank and Alice as witnesses.

The judge looked at Megan with so much love, it was palpable. "It is with great pleasure for me to do what should have already been done two years ago. Megan, are you absolutely sure that you want Jeff and Hope to be your parents?"

Without hesitation, "Yes please, I do your Honor, sir. One request before we start, please...."

They all looked puzzled.

"Your honor sir, I would like to change my name...." She looked at everyone and said. "I've decided that I like the name my mother was going to give me, Gypsy Rose...."

"That's a beautiful name...." Hope said with a smile. "It suits you perfectly!"

The judge smiled and nodded to the clerk to change the paperwork. "Gypsy Rose it will be."

It only took a couple of minutes for the clerk to return with the corrected paperwork.

"Okay are we ready?" Everyone nodded. "Jeff and Hank, you both risked your lives to rescue Gypsy, and we are so grateful that you were successful."

"I'd do it all again," said Hank.

"Me too," agreed Jeff.

The judge smiled lovingly at the two men. He knew they meant every word. He then turned to the women, "Hope and Alice, your roles as liaisons, although less dangerous, was vital to their success. I commend you both."

They said in unison, "Thank you."

"Before I make this official, Gypsy," he smiled first, then with the utmost respect, he began to scold her, "I want you to understand how dangerous it is for you to heal humans. Unless, of course, someone's life depends on it like Mary did that day. You must stick to animals. Do you understand?"

"Yes, I understand. I never wanted to heal people in the first place."

"Yes, I know, but you will help people in need. I just want you to be very careful when you do."

Gypsy smiled shyly, "Yes, sir. I will try."

The judge laid a piece of paper on the table. Gypsy if you will sign here. Jeff and Hope sign on these two lines, please."

When everyone signed the document, the judge signed the bottom. A notary took the paper and affixed her stamp. Once she had completed the process, the judge turned to Hank and Alice. "I have a request from Gypsy. She would like for you both to be her god parents. Is that okay with you?"

"Oh Yes! We would be honored. If it's okay with Jeff and Hope…?"

"Are you kidding me!" Jeff exclaimed. "Of course, it's okay! It's perfect in fact!"

"Okay then, that's settled." The judge was pleased. "Hank and Alice normally this is done in a church by a clergyman and lucky for you all, I am an ordained minister, too. If you will sign on these two lines."

They did and Gypsy hugged them both, "After living with my mother, you have no idea how much it means to me to be with people who really love me. And Judge Sir and Mary, the only people I'm missing are Grandparents. Would you mind being mine?"

"Child," whimpered Mary. "That would be an honor and a blessing to us! Thank you!"

Chapter Twenty
Ten Years Later

Jeff and Gypsy boarded the plane in Florida and laid back in their seats. This trip to Dr. Jenkins would be her last; he was ill. According to him, he only had a month or two left. I wanted to try and heal him, but he said no; too late. Which is why we met him at his home. He gave us all my medical records. The last thing he wanted was someone to find them and exploit me. Now that she was nestled in her seat, she the exact conversation.

"Thanks, Doc, for the documents. I'm so grateful that you looked after me all these years and I'm going to miss my trips to see you. However, I will not miss this humidity."

He chuckled, "No I suppose not." He paused, "Gypsy, there's something I need to tell you."

I frowned, "Okay…what?"

He looked at Jeff, he nodded. "Here's the bottom line. You are immortal, which means all of the family you've accepted will die in the near future."

"Yes, I know. I'm hoping that someone from my kind will find me."

"And if they don't?"

She stared at him dumbfounded, "They talk to me all the time! I'm never alone. I'm certain that one of them will want to find me."

"That's interesting. Did you tell me that before?"

"No, probably not. I didn't think anyone would believe me or they would think I was Schizophrenic like my mother."

"Well, since no one has showed up yet, I wanted to guarantee that at least your family for a bit longer than normal." He paused to drink water and thought, *here goes.* "Remember when you were in the hospital in Florida, and we took all the blood from you?"

"Yes…"

"I had never seen anyone like you before and I was fascinated by the prospect that you were immortal. So… I made a serum out of most of that blood we took. And when Jeff, Hope and you came the next time, I gave Jeff and Hope a shot of that serum. I took some more blood this time and I'm going to have a doctor friend of mine run it through the lab at the hospital. I want to see if there is any change in Jeff's blood. What I'm hoping for is that his body will be taken to the serum and he and Hope could probably live another 50 years or longer. I'll call you with the results. What do you think?"

"Of course I love the idea, but won't that doctor get suspicious?"

"The doctor thinks it's just one of my routine blood draws. My wife will pick up the results just like always."

"The lab technician?"

"I'm looking at the RH factor number. Most techs don't even know what that is for."

"Okay, let us know. How long before we get the results back?"

"A day or two."

"We will be waiting for your call."

As she stared out the window, she couldn't believe that Jeff and Hope went along with the doctor's experiment. She asked him, "Jeff, why did you and Hope let the doctor experiment on you?"

He took ahold of her hand. "Easy, you were only ten at the time and we thought that the serum would make sure we were around longer to help you. We figured out long ago that you might not be completely human. The doctor only confirmed our suspicions."

"I see...."

"We just wanted to make sure that you weren't alone to soon. And hey, this might not even work."

She returned to staring out the window.

The doctor called in two days as promised. "There is a definite boost in the RH factor counts. I think it worked!"

Jeff and Hope were beyond thrilled. Even though they couldn't tell anyone why, not even Hank or Alice. After a few weeks, it was like nothing ever happened. Nonmales set in that is until one Friday morning.

Gypsy left her tiny apartment heading to the feed store to open up for Alice. She was pregnant with her third child and a bit nauseous. Hope was keeping an eye on Alice's while making breakfast for Jeff, Hank and the kids. Hank wanted to take care of the young ones so Alice could sleep. Jeff was going to the warehouse to bring more bales of hay and seed sacks. Stocking the store for spring planting was essential for every farmer in this county. This is the only large animal feed store within fifty miles and they better have enough supplies for the sixty-plus farms within the area.

Gypsy was delighted to lend a hand as she loved the smell of the feed store. It was probably the hay bales stacked all around the walls, that fresh hay smell made her think of the farm and how much she missed it. Besides, she could study the plans for her vet clinic that was being built next door. Hank and Jeff were nearly finished with putting on the new red metal roof. The interior was over half-finished, and she had to admit her excitement was growing.

When she pulled up to the store, she had a strange feeling, but chalked it off to the dark windows. Hank always had the lights on, and the coffee made when she arrived. Alice must be really sick. *Once I turn on the lights and make the coffee, it will feel better.*

The early hours passed quickly, the farmers who wanted an early start in the fields, kept her busy. Finally, the store was quiet, she was pouring a stale cup of coffee when she heard the doorbell jingle. She stepped out of the storeroom to see who it was. A young man was standing in the middle of the isle. Gypsy sucked in a deep breath. He was strikingly handsome and when he saw her, he smiled.

"I've been looking for you for a very long time," he said calmly.

Gypsy wasn't sure she heard him correctly. "Excuse me.... what did you say?"

"I've been looking for you...."

"Why?"

He held out his hand. "Give me your hand please."

She just stared at him.

"I'm sure you'll understand once you do."

"Do you have a name?"

"I apologize, my name is Caleb."

She went over to the table by the register and sat down. She motioned for him to sit, which he did. "Okay Caleb, what is this all about?"

Several customers came in about that time and she waited on them before returning to the table. "Sorry for the interruption."

He held out his hand once again. "It's too hard to explain. Please take my hand."

"I want to warn you, I can and will turn you into dust if you try to hurt me!"

He smiled sheepishly, "I have no doubt."

She looked into his eyes, and noticed they were the same violet eyes as hers. She was startled and stood up so she could back away.

Why hadn't I noticed them before? I should have.... He's like me, he's one of my kind.

She went back to the table, sat down, and took hold of his hand. Instantly, images flashed before her eyes, all of them in other worlds, fighting battles, and one thing was clear, Caleb was her mate. She whispered through tears of remembering, "are these re-incarnations? Past lives?"

"Yes, of sorts."

Her tears were slowing down enough that she could speak. "I'm sorry I don't recognize you, although you are familiar somehow."

"That's okay. It will take a little while for you to remember me...., but you will."

Gypsy didn't know what to think. He was so much like her, in so many ways. He had a large build, rugged, sturdy, and formidable.

Several customers burst in, the ones that use their lunch hour to purchase small items they forgot to get or just discovered they needed. Each one, hoping to find that item in ten seconds or less, so they can get back to work on time. The last customer left and when Gypsy turned around Caleb was gone. Loneliness crept in, she missed the connection to him, a feeling she had never known. No one has ever touched her heart like he just had.

She made a fresh pot of coffee and took a cup over to the table. What in the hell happened? A better question is, was any of it real? Caleb felt real, but was he? Or did I just envision him? Why did he go? A better question, will he return?

Jeff was standing in front of her and when she looked up, she jumped. "How long have you been standing there?"

"Awhile. Where were you just now?"

"Daydreaming...."

"About a handsome gentleman that's inspecting the construction site?"

"Maybe…. dad, his name is Caleb and he's like me."

"Like you how?"

"We came from the same place. I'm not sure where that place is just yet. I actually thought I dreamt him up. But your saying he's at the construction site!"

"Yes….and where did he come from?"

"I have no idea, he walked through the front door and said he's been looking for me."

Jeff sat down. *I wonder if this is one of the people she said she heard talking to her when she was ten? He had noticed how sullen she was lately, and he was pretty sure she was quite lonely. I just don't want her to get hurt.*

"I'm going to relieve Hank for a bit. When he gets here, you go out and visit with Caleb."

She grinned from ear to ear, "Yes, I will."

The blush that was appearing on her cheeks made Jeff happy. *Our little girl is all grown up!* Over his shoulder, he said, "Have him stay for dinner."

He wants to check him out, she thought but said, "I'll ask him."

Gypsy impatiently anticipated Hank's arrival. While she waited, her mind wandered back to the visions Caleb showed her. One in particular stood out, the scene where she was battling a creature that looked familiar to her. It looked like the mythological creatures from her schoolbooks. A time when Merlin the Magician reigned, and magic was practiced everywhere. How she loved the Fables, and often dreamt that she was there living a magical life. In Caleb's vision, she was riding something that had wings. There was a forked spear in her hand, and she was chasing something important. She tried so hard to bring the whole vision forward but failed. *Patience,* she thought, *patience....*

The doorbell jingled and she stood to see who was coming in. Strangers, a man, and a woman.

"Can I help you?" Gypsy felt suddenly sick. The back door opened, and Hank came in.

He assessed that Gypsy wasn't feeling well. "Something you folks need?"

"No, a question or two is all."

"Certainly, fire away...."

The woman was shy and barely spoke above a whisper, "We are looking for Hope Olsen, she's, my sister. We heard she was living in these parts."

"Wait here....," replied Hank, to Gypsy, he said, "watch the store, please."

"Of course...." She turned to them, "Can I offer you some tea or coffee?"

The man spoke for both of them, "Green tea would be wonderful, if you have it."

"We do." She picked up her cup off the table. "Please have a seat. It won't take long; the water is already hot!"

"Thank you....," they all but collapsed at the table.

Gypsy brought cups, sugar, fresh crème, and a teapot of boiling water to the table. She laid the tea bags on the saucers. She went to the refrigerator to get butter and then to the cupboard for napkins. The bread was in the breadbox.

"Here's some soda bread and freshly churned butter, all homemade by my mum. She makes the best bread and butter in the county."

At that moment, Hope came running through the loading dock opening. "Sarah and Tim, how did you get here?"

"Horse and buggy. They're outside!"

Gypsy's eyes widened. She leapt up and ran for the door.

"What just happened?" Sarah asked.

"My daughter is a vet and...."

Sarah turned to look towards the closing door. "That woman is Gypsy?"

"Yes...."

Gypsy now understood why she felt sick when they came in. It was coming from their horse! She rounded the corner and found the horse detached from the cart. His head was down and there was froth in his mouth. She ran the few yards to lay her hands on his neck and began chanting. The horse whinnied softly, and she looked up to see Caleb watching her.

"He has choke!" She said, embarrassed that he was watching her so intently.

"Yes, I know. They've been traveling for over a month with very little rest. I've healed his feet, and I was about to take care of the choke when you came out."

Not sure she heard him correctly, she asked, "You healed his feet?"

"Yes....is that a problem?"

"No! I didn't know there was another like me.... I am so grateful...." Relief flooded through her, and she began to cry.

Caleb took her in his arms and held her until he knew she was okay. "Have a seat on the running board. I want to finish with his feet."

"I'm fine now. He needs water and good hay. I'll get those from the store."

"A trough would be better," informed Caleb.

"True, we have one in the barn, but until he's completely healed, I'd rather let him stand for a couple of hours. His legs are hard as rocks from being over worked. We'll put him in a stall tonight. I'll be right back."

Caleb only nodded. As he watched her run to the store, he knew he was finally home. His search was over and now he could rest. A tear trickled down his cheek and he quickly wiped it away.

With the horse bedded down for the night, Caleb and Gypsy headed into the house for dinner.

Chapter Twenty-One
The Abduction

Attached to Hank's Feed & Grain stood a newly built red and white fully functional veterinary hospital. The sign over the door reads: Rose's Animal Hospital. From the day of the grand opening, the hospital has been extremely busy. Word spread like wildfire across the county, that Gypsy and her new husband, Caleb, were devoted veterinarians.

Life couldn't be better, she thought. *Caleb was perfect, and the clinic was booming.* It was Friday morning and Caleb left early to go the clinic. He had a complicated surgery scheduled and he wanted to be prepared. Two hours later Gypsy opened the back door to the clinic, Caleb was not there. Maybe he's over at the store, but when she walked up to the loading dock, the store was dark.

She scanned Hope and Alice's houses, in the big bay window at Alice's house, she could see Hope and Alice making breakfast. She unlocked the back door of the store and entered. No one….so where is Caleb? Hank? Jeff?

Caleb, can you hear me? No response. *Caleb, answer me, please!* Still no response. The store and the clinic are supposed to open in thirty minutes! She picked up the phone and called Alice.

When she answered, Gypsy, trying to sound cheerful, asked, "Good morning. Do you know where Jeff or Hank are by chance?"

"Good morning to you too. But to tell the truth, I haven't seen either of them this morning, I slept late, and Hank was already gone. I thought he went to the store."

"No, they're not here. Did they have a pickup or delivery this morning?"

"I honestly don't know. I'm sure they're around somewhere. I be over in time to open the store."

"Okay, thanks Alice."

She hung up and walked over to the clinic. She unlocked the door, and thought, *they'd turn up soon. They've just lost track of time.* She fed and watered the few animals she had, cleaned their cages and, although they weren't dirty, she washed the dust off the pet runs.

Every Friday morning from 9am to 11am was reserved for vaccines and immunizations. By the time she finished the inside chores, customers and their pets were lining up out front. *I might as well get started.*

The morning flew by. When the last patient left, she locked the door and went to the store.

Alice and Hope were pacing. It looked like Hope was on the verge of hysteria!

Gypsy asked, "Have you heard anything from the guys?"

"No," said Alice. "And I'm really worried. Does Caleb have any idea where they went?"

"No, I haven't seen Caleb since he left the house this morning! His car is here, but he isn't. You don't think something's happen to them, do you?"

The two women just stared at her. Hope said softly, "I didn't think so, but…."

"But what?" Alice was starting to panic.

"Jeff got a threatening note two months ago from Hopkins' brother. But Jeff said not to worry. So, I didn't."

"Do you still have the note?" asked Alice.

"I don't know, but I'm sure he would never throw it away. I'll go look." With panic written all over her face, Hope ran for the house and returned within five minutes waving the note.

They moved to the table and sat down. Hope began to read....

Jeff Olsen, you are directly responsible for Jerry's death, and I will make you pay in ways you never knew existed. My brother was torn apart by wolves because you lured him out there and you had the wolves kill him! Harold

"There is a drawing of a dead man."

"I think we should call the constable and show him all this," said Alice.

"Yes," agreed Hope and Gypsy.

Gypsy kept her eye on the clinic. "I have to go to the clinic, a client is pulling in. Keep me informed…"

"Certainly….and Gypsy, the police will want to talk to you too."

Gypsy paused for a split second. "Yes, I suppose they will."

Alice made the call to the police. It seemed like she just hung up and the officer was walking through the door. "That was quick. I guess there's not much happening around here."

Hope was taken back by Alice's sharp tone and sarcastic remark but said nothing because Officer Chapman walked in.

He was polite and attentive as we answered his millions of questions. Such as names, ages, descriptions and did we have a current photograph?

"No… I don't think so. But maybe Gypsy has the picture the judge took at her adoption…."

Hope's eyes lit up! "I have a copy…. I'll be right back."

"While we wait, I could interview your neighbors on the boardwalk."

"Yes, please talk to all of them. We'll be here. Oh and, Gypsy's shop is right next door."

He nodded and left. Alice started shaking valiantly. Realization was setting in; Hank could be already dead! Her mind started spinning out of control and would have had not Hope walked through the door in time to catch Alice before she hit the floor.

"Oh no, Alice! Alice….!" The instant Alice was safely laying on the floor, she ran over to Gypsy's and burst through the door and screamed, "Gypsy! Alice collapsed! Hurry!"

Hope heard, "I'll be right there…"

Gypsy handed the vaccinated Calico kitten back to its owner, "See you in three weeks."

The lady smiled, "Thank you, Doctor."

Gypsy locked her shop and ran to the feed store. Alice lay flat on the floor; her breathing was shallow, and she was white as a ghost.

Gypsy started checking her over. "What happened?"

"Honestly Gypsy, I don't know. When I came back, she was in free fall. I'm just glad I caught her before her head hit the floor. She certainly would have died."

Gypsy didn't respond as she had begun to chant. Always in the same foreign language and her forehead resting in her hands that were on Alice's chest. Watching her work her magic on someone was like watching a miracle.

Alice opened her eyes, "What happened?" and she tried to sit up.

Gypsy held her in place, "Not just yet. Give yourself a chance to wake up fully."

Hope nearly in tears said, "You fainted."

"Fainted! Me!" and this time she did sit up.

Gypsy smiled, "Take it easy momma. I've got to get back to the clinic. See you in a bit...."

Realization spread across her face... "What? No!"

"Alice that's wonderful!" squealed Hope.

Alice was clearly stunned. Officer Chapman returned involved in writing his notes, not paying attention that the women were seated on the floor. "Okay, I think I have all I need to get started. And I promise I'll keep you posted." He looked up. "Did something happen?"

"Alice fainted...," said Hope. "She's okay now."

"Let's get her off the floor." He bent down scooped her up like she was a two-year-old and put her in the chair."

Alice blushed, "Thank you."

He patted her shoulder, "You're welcome. Now I need to go next door and talk to Gypsy."

"Okay, thanks officer."

With a nod, he was gone.

An hour later, the clinic was closed for the day and Gypsy went back to the feed store only to find Hope and Alice still at the table. They looked like frozen statues.

Gypsy quietly sat down and saw the terrified look on both their faces. "Don't worry, Caleb will contact me the instant he feels they're safe."

"How?" whimpered Alice.

"Caleb and I use mental telepathy to communicate these days...."

Hope whispered, "We figured it was something like that cause we rarely hear either of you speak out loud anymore."

"I didn't realize that it was noticeable."

"Well, others might not notice, but we're family, we notice."

"I guess so...., I want to assure you that Caleb is so much stronger than I. He will contact me as soon as he can."

"Um, I hate to ask you, but will you stay with us tonight?" Hope asked.

"Of course I will, mom," she reassured her. "I won't leave you.... I didn't realize how hungry I was. I'm sure you are too. Let's close up and go to the house."

Hope leaped up heading to lock the front door. Gypsy went over to the register to close out the day's receipts. Alice stayed seated, her eyes were glazed over, her mind obviously lost in the nightmare of her missing husband and now another baby on the way.

Shock...thought Gypsy. We'll let her rest until we're finished closing up.

Hope and Sarah cooked a light meal of pea soup and soda bread with fresh butter, both grateful to have something to do. As it turned out, no one was really hungry. They ate in silence and immediately cleaned up the kitchen. One by one they disappeared into their rooms; sobbing was the only sound that could be heard throughout the house.

Gypsy went outside to clear her mind. She had to think and try to get some perspective. Events weren't adding up. Why now after all these years. More baffling was why they took Caleb. He wasn't involved in Hopkin's murder, unless he was over at the store when they came in. Wrong place, wrong time? Maybe.... but why didn't he banish them? He has the power to do that. Maybe, they already had Jeff and Hank tied up or knocked out! He would've gone to protect them.... but then again, he could easily disarm them. The only way they could subdue him is render him unconscious somehow! A lump formed in her throat.

She didn't know how long she had sat there staring at his car, willing it to tell her where he was. Nothing but silence, so just before dawn she went inside to lay down because nothing more was going to happen tonight.

Chapter Twenty-Two
Buried

Caleb opened his eyes, it was pitch black, and after listening for a while there was no sound, not even a bird or a car driving by. The worst part was the feeling of no space around him, claustrophobia.

"What happened?"

As hard as he tried to recall the chain of events, it was clear there were a few pieces missing. No sense in trying to figure that out now, he thought and tried to move. All tied up, he chuckled as he released his bondages with a single flick of his finger.

"Easy enough," he said to no one.

He yelled, "Hank? Jeff?" No response, so he laid still, reaching out with his mind. *Hank or Jeff if you can hear me speak out loud. I will hear you.* He waited, nothing. Repeating the mantra several times, he finally heard a groan. *Hank, is that you?* Groan again. *Wake up! I need you to talk to me.* Time ticked by slowly, then all of a sudden, he heard a terrifying scream. "Caleb!"

Okay Hank, you need to calm down and tell me about your surroundings.

"I'm buried alive!"

Caleb thought, *me too*! "Hank don't worry, I'll keep you in oxygen. Then I'm going to get out of here so I can find you, okay?"

"Okay," was his weak reply.

"Tell me when you can feel the air coming in..." A minute or two passed by before he heard, "I feel it."

"Great!"

Now to get myself out of here. It seemed like forever before he heard the sound of the whirlwind. Once he felt the wind pounding on the box, he stopped the wind and popped up the lid.

He was free! Now to find Hank. He looked all around for a mound of freshly turned soil. Widening his circle, with every lap, nothing.

Picking up a broken branch, he called out, "Hank, I'm going to start hitting trees. Tell me when you hear me, okay?"

"Okay, um, I was bounced around in some sort of hurricane a few minutes ago."

Caleb looked up. Dangling eighty feet off the ground in a tree was a wooden box on a thin rope. How did they get him up there? *I don't know if I can get him down...*

Hank, do you feel like you're standing or on your head?

"I think standing."

Okay, I'm going to bring you down now.

"No...there is a bomb in here."

Is there a timer?

"Yes..."

Tell me when the time goes off... Caleb closed his eyes to picture the timer and its electrical components. One by one, in his mind, he pictured each wire and where it might lead. *Can you see the colors of the wires, Hank.*

"No...just the timer..."

Keep your eye on that timer.

"Um, Caleb there's only one minute left!"

Plenty of time. Caleb tried to assure him. Okay, here we go. Yellow, red, then black! Yank!

Hank yelled! "The timer stopped."

Closing his eyes once again, he untied the rope. Hoping, beyond hope, he could hold the box and the giant man with his mind. Slowly, he lowered the box. Halfway down, the box started to shake and spin slightly.

Hank stay still...Hank stop...no response. Maybe he's unconscious...seizures! The box started to come down rapidly. Caleb tried to slow it down and succeeded slightly. The box hit the ground hard and splintered on impact.

The explosion was loud and echoed painfully in Caleb's ears. He ran to Hank, who was thrown clear when the box broke, and started dragging him into the woods. No doubt whoever set the bomb will be coming here any minute. Caleb sent a quick message to Gypsy that he and Hank were fine, but he had no idea as to where they were. Jeff's where-a-bouts were still unknown.

Footfalls could be heard running toward the explosion area. As soon as they ran passed Caleb, he grabbed Hank again and continued to drag him further into the woods. *I must find a safe place to hide until I can assess Hank's injuries.*

There were a half a dozen fallen trees thrown haphazardly against a knoll. Caleb crawled underneath and began to pull Hank inside. The sunlight was fading but Caleb could easily see that Hank had serious injuries. He put his hands on his chest and began the mantra in his native language. Halfway through, he put his forehead on top of his hands and continued his healing.

"Come on Hank...wake up...," he wasn't sure if the healing worked completely. If he doesn't wake up in five minutes, I'll do it again. Raising the dead is easier than putting body parts back together.

Off in the distance, he heard voices. They weren't getting closer, but they sounded like they were searching for us. He heard the word footprints. *Drag marks!* Caleb went outside and looked at the ground to see if there were any leading into the safety zone. There were! He found branch fronds and began sweeping the ground for as far back as he dared. He also made sure that he didn't leave any tracks that could lead them to Hank.

Chapter Twenty-Three
El Guardo's

Gypsy sat straight up. Caleb was telling her that he and Hank were ok, but Jeff was still missing. As relieved as I am, the idea of telling Hope that Jeff was still missing disturbs me more. For now, I'll keep quiet until they find Jeff, but I've got to go home where I can think clearly.

"Hope, I have to go home and get clean clothes. I'll be back."

"Okay see you later."

At home, she threw off her clinic clothes, showered, and grabbed a sweatshirt and jeans. *I have to find them. Caleb...are you okay?*

Yes...

How's Hank?

Stable for the most part.

Okay good. I'll see if I can find you.

No, we're fine. Go after them.

Are you sure?

I have no idea where we are. You'd be wasting precious time. Find them Gypsy before they go after Hope and Alice, they know we escaped.

What can you tell me about the men who captured you?

Not much, I was injected with some kind of drug that knocked me out. But I'm sure one was Jerry's brother because he kept repeating, this is for Jerry. He sounded crazed out of his mind.

Okay, I'm going into town and see if I can find them.

Be careful....

I will...

While Jeff was in Florida, Clive mentioned that we should try a restaurant named El Guano's. He went on and on about how much he and Hopkins loved the place. I'll start there. Pulling into the restaurant parking lot, she sees three men, covered in dirt, enter the restaurant. *Could I be this lucky? Of course not, these three men could be farmers just as easily as a hundred other hard-working professions.*

She waited several minutes before entering. The threesome was sitting at a large round table in the middle of the room. She took a small table a few feet away and put her back to them. As she buried her face in the menu, she is keeping one ear on their conversation.

Pictures of plated food lined both sides of the menu. She chose something called enchiladas and a taco combo plate. To drink, she ordered a coke, something she never had before.

The waitress took her order and returned in seconds with chips, salsa, and the coke to wash it down. The coke had bubbles! Every time she tried to take a drink; the bubbles went up her nose! *How did they make the bubbles and why haven't they stopped? There's nothing on the bottom of the glass or inside that could make them! A real mystery.*

Oddly enough, she noticed, that the men were sullen and not talking much. Their meal came and they ate in silence. When their plates were cleared, the smallest of the men said, "How do you think they got away?"

"No idea," the biggest one said. "But nothing surprises me when it comes to those folks."

"True enough," said the guy in the plaid shirt.

The big guy, who Gypsy was sure was the brother, Harold said, "At least we still have the bastard that had my brother killed."

"How long do you think he can last in that pit?"

"Couple of days or even a week on the outside that is if he even wakes up. That was a hard fall."

Plaid shirt says, "I'll go out and check him when we're finished eating while it's still light."

Gypsy's heart sank, she reached out to Caleb, *he's in a pit somewhere!*

If you can follow him, I will help you lift him, then you can grab him and drive like crazy to get way. Just don't get caught. I'd hate for you to have to fight him.

Caleb, he can't hurt me; nobody can.

That's what I thought too…

You do have a point. I'll contact you when I have him.

The food was exquisite, with so many spicy flavors and rich textures. I'll have to remember this place. I've never experienced any food that was so flavorful. She finished her dinner, paid the bill, and left before them. Now to position myself to follow plaid shirt.

She didn't have to wait long. The three men came out and made plans to meet later tonight at a place called, Hammer's Pub.

At least I'll know where they will be. I'll let Officer Chapman round them up once I make sure Jeff is safe.

Mr. Plaid shirt was easy to follow. He sang country songs so loud that people in the next county could follow him. All of a sudden, he turned down a trail that his truck barely fit. She went a short distance and turned into a cutout in the road. Turning off the engine, she got out and softly ran back to the entrance to the path.

His truck was five hundred feet down the path. She listened carefully to hear footfalls to find out in which direction he went. For what seemed like forever, she finally heard his voice off in the distance. He was hollering at someone. *That's it, buddy, keep hollering.*

It was getting dark as she approached. She was careful not to get close enough that he could hear her.

Go away! I need to get him out of there…

In a few minutes, he replaced a lid over the hole. Satisfied that Jeff was still in the hole, he turned around to head back to his truck. Gypsy laid flat against the ground, until she heard the truck engine start up and back out. The instant she heard him take off down the road, she leapt up and ran to the hole. There was a wooden lid across the opening which she instantly removed. Jeff lay at the bottom of a deep rock well and he was on his side.

"Jeff, can you hear me?" No response and no movement. "I'm going to lift you out now."

She took hold of the edge of the stone rim. Laying her head in her hands, she began to chant softly. Inch by inch, Jeff began to rise, but at ten to twelve feet, his weight pulled him down about a foot or so. It was getting hard to hold him let alone keep lifting him. Time after time he slipped down a foot or two at a time and she was getting tired of trying to hold his weight.

Fear crept in as she felt her grasp threatening to let him go. "Caleb! Help me! I'm losing him!" She felt a sudden surge of strength! "Yes!"

Even with Caleb's help, it seemed like forever before she got him out. She laid him down on the ground, replaced the lid, and ran for her car. She backed in and managed to get him in the backseat. Hospital first or should she stop somewhere to heal him?

"Caleb, I have him!"

"Is he alive?"

"I don't know. I'm afraid to stop to find out."

"I think you had better find somewhere to find out, maybe an alley or parking lot somewhere."

"Okay...I'll let you know..."

The restaurant where she had dinner was coming up. That would be a perfect place as they wouldn't be coming back there. She pulled in and went around back. Opening the back door where his head lay, she felt a pulse. Yes! Faint but there. Laying her hands on his shoulder, she began to chant. Finally, he groaned.

"Thank you!"

Caleb he's alive!

Great! Now find a hospital. Don't heal him, the police need to see him as he is. You can heal him later.

Got it...then I will come to find you.

Yes, yes...

Finding the hospital was easy as it was on Main Street. She ran in and started yelling for help. They got him out of the car and onto a gurney, they whisked him away. A nurse came out and asked a ton of questions.

"I need you to call Officer Chapman in Flatbush, immediately. Tell him to get here as fast as possible."

The nurse left and Gypsy felt it was okay to call Alice and Hope to tell them the men were okay and safe. She found a pay phone and dialed.

Alice answered. "I'll explain everything later, all you both need to know is that Jeff and Hank are safe. Jeff is in Holland hospital in Hamilton. He is being operated. I'm going to go and pick up Hank and Caleb. I promise to call you the instant I hear anything about their condition."

"Thank you, thank you…"

Gypsy hung up and by the time she got back to her seat, Officer Chapman was walking in the door. He looks like someone's grandpa, late fifties, silver hair, great smile and kind eyes. Gypsy stood up, he saw her and came directly toward her. She filled him in and included where the men were going to meet up at Hammer's Pub.

She also explained, "We need to find Hank and Caleb immediately. Hank is hurt too!"

He sat still for a long minute before he said, "Logic tells me that they put all three men together or in close proximity to each other. It doesn't make sense to spread them out. Can you take me to where you found Jeff?"

"Yes, I can. Let's go!"

Hope and Alice came running in just as they were about to leave. Chapman said, "I had a squad car bring them here."

"Thank you…" Gypsy went over to them at the nurse's station. "I'll be back as soon as I can with Hank and Caleb. Stay here and if you can't, tell the nurse where you will be. Okay?"

"Yes, go!"

Chapman drove so Gypsy could direct him. When they got close, she had him slow down so she could see the entrance to the path.

"You weren't kidding when you said path."

"No, I wasn't."

"I don't think this squad car can get in there."

"I parked in a cutout just up the road."

"I think I'm going to pull across the entrance and turn on the hazards. Let's go." He handed her a flashlight.

She took him to the hole where they put Jeff. Chapman called for a forensic team to come out to their location.

While they waited, Gypsy contacted Caleb. We are here in the vicinity of where we think you are. Describe to me your surroundings.

"A half a dozen fallen trees against a small hill. It's dark, will you be able to find us?"

"Yes, I think so. How's Hank?"

"I don't have a good understanding of the human body like you do, so I'm not sure."

**It never occurred to her that he didn't know the human body. Where has he been all his life? Something I will have to ask him later. Okay we will find you, don't worry.

We?

Officer Chapman and I, he's helping me find you. In fact, he thinks he knows about where you are. Right now, we're waiting for a forensic team to get here, and they are pulling up now.

A voice came out of the radio. "We have arrested all three. They are in custody."

Caleb came out. They have arrested all of them. Start yelling.

Caleb scrambled out from under the tree and stood up. "We're over here!"

Chapman and Gypsy both turned toward the sound of Caleb's voice.

"We hear you, yell again."

Gypsy started to run. Again Caleb...

He yelled again and Gypsy changed direction slightly. *Again...*

He yelled again and again until Gypsy shone the flashlight in his face. She ran to him and hugged him until he convinced her that he was alright. They grabbed hold of Hank and dragged him out. Chapman showed up and he lifted Hank like he was a child, threw him over his shoulder, and ran. He called for another ambulance.

Chapman made Caleb ride in the ambulance so they could check him over too. Once they were at the hospital, Gypsy and Chapman went out to the lobby to get Alice. With everyone found and safe, Gypsy slumped in a chair, relief flooded her, and she began to cry. Grateful for the best outcome possible.

Chapman and the forensic team took a million pictures and fingerprints of their captive places, they collected all the rope and wood, and the hole where Jeff was buried was photographed extensively. Caleb's grave site went through a forensic collection of soil samples and the wooden box. All of it was taken back to the lab.

Alice ran the store while Hope nursed the men. Neither man was critically injured, Hank a broken leg and Jeff had a puncture spleen so they were fairly easy. They agreed that with the police and lawyers constantly about, it would not be a good idea for Gypsy to instantly heal them. The hard part was trying to keep them down. These are two very active men and laying around was not comfortable for either of them.

With Caleb's help, Tim and Sarah's house was nearly finished. They were to the point where Tim could put in the cabinets and hook up the faucets.

Two weeks later, Officer Chapman returned with the results of the forensic analysis. He had questions. A lot of questions.

"Good evening, everyone. I have results of the forensic evidence, but first I want to tell you that Harold and his buddies confessed to kidnapping. what that means to you, is that there will not be a trial and they will not see the light of day in their lifetime."

Jeff asked, "So, this harassment is over. No one else is left to crawl out of the woodwork?"

Chapman shook his head. "Not to my knowledge, no."

"Okay...continue."

"The forensics report does not disagree with your account of what happened. Having said that there are questions as to how you, Caleb were able to free Hank."

Caleb knew this was going to create problems. After careful thought there is no way he will believe any fabricated story so he told the truth. "I levitated him to the ground."

Chapman stuttered, "You did?"

"Yes, sir, I did."

"Ah, how do you do that?"

"With my mind…"

"I see," it was clear Chapman wasn't expecting that answer, "can you demonstrate?"

Caleb didn't say a word, he just lifted the officer out of his chair and hung him from the ceiling. He then returned him to his chair. "Like that."

"Okay…." He just sat and looked at Caleb for the longest time. Finally, he said, "The grave where you were buried. How did you get out?"

"I created a strong whirlwind that removed the dirt and then I simply removed the lid."

"Simply uh."

"Yes, nails are of no consequence to me."

"There not?"

Caleb answered flatly, "No sir. They're not."

"Um care to demonstrate the whirlwind?"

"Sure, let's go outside."

They all went out to the field behind the barn. Caleb closed his eyes, and a whirlwind began to form. Caleb kept concentrating until the whirlwind was throwing dirt all over the place. Then he opened his eyes which stopped the whole thing. "Just like that."

Chapman was befuddled but not startled. "I get it. Thank you for your time, folks. I'll be going now." And he walked over to his car, got in and drove away.

Gypsy whispered, "What do you think will happen now that you told the truth?"

"I don't know. I was going to try and give other explanations as to how I did all that, but I couldn't think of anything that would work. So, I told the truth. They knew Hank was hanging eighty feet off the ground. There's no other explanation than what I told him."

"You're right… there isn't. I wonder what he's going to tell them back at the station."

"They have the forensics. They had proved that the only feasible answers are the ones I told them."

"True." She hugged him even tighter. "I'm starved, let's eat! How about Chinese?"

The End

www.ingramcontent.com/pod-product-compliance
Lightning Source LLC
LaVergne TN
LVHW040138080526
838202LV00042B/2958